Spirit of the Season

Brian Lamont

Published by Penbury Press
21 (fl) Morningside Place, Edinburgh, EH10 5ES

E-mail: penburypress@yahoo.co.uk
Facebook: Penbury Press

Amazon Kindle edition 2012.
Printed by CreateSpace.

ISBN-13: 978-1523763481
ISBN-10: 1523763485

Except ye see signs and wonders, ye will not believe.

John, 4:48

To Larissa
(for believing)

One

In an age long past, when homes were lit with soft yellow flames and warmed by the heat from wood fires, there was a candle maker who lived in a cottage beyond a small village, set on the edge of a deep forest.

The candle maker had learned his trade as a child, watching his father in his workshop melting pots of beeswax above a furnace. When the wax was melted, his father would lay flaxen wicks over wooden poles and carefully dip them into the hot fluid, over and over again, to build them up into the perfect round sticks that were hung to set on the iron ceiling hooks above. Then there were the moulds that were filled to make candles for the glass chandeliers in the big houses on the estates, and those for the churches that were lighted in all their services, ceremonies and celebrations throughout the year. The candle maker's work was found in homes across the region, from the tiny lodge of a shepherd to the sprawling manor of a lord, and it was the same light that entered their homes, whether they were grand or simple, as it came from the same man.

Hidden away on the outskirts of the village, the candle maker was nervous of visitors and had grown up apart from other children. It was said that he had the look of his mother, with his round moon face, piercing blue eyes and long golden curls of hair. He never went to the local school but instead worked with his father, and delivered their goods to the provisions store in the village and the cottages in the outlying district. Once a year, in autumn, he would take a little handcart around the nearby homes and farms that kept beehives to buy wax for his father. He also visited the far off monastery, where monks produced the finest wax and worked in harmony with their brothers' chants, which sounded out from the cloister. When he was not working, he would spend hours alone watching the insects, plants and creatures of the forest, and he gained a thoughtful way about him, as he came to know how a day passed into night and the seasons changed the world about him.

In spring, newborn lambs covered the meadow. There were bluebells on the ground, blossom was on the trees and mayflies filled the air. In summer, crops were in the fields, fish basked in the river and the smell of baking bread was found in every home. Autumn was the time for apples, and nuts and leaves covered the forest floor. It was a time for wandering in fields of tall-stemmed blue flowers, and pulling flax to dry and spin into candlewicks. In winter, however, the world went to sleep.

For three months of the year, it seemed, nature slept, while people were awake and their homes surrounded by ice and snow. Nature provided throughout the other seasons, but in winter people had to look after themselves. In late autumn, they stocked their barns, larders and store cupboards, and piled chopped wood by the door, for if not their animals would starve and they too would go hungry in the cold. Winter brought shorter days and long nights, and without candles or lanterns they could not go far from their homes and would dwell in the dark with no light in their lives.

The chandler's boy, as he came to be known, had the happiest childhood imaginable, even though there were no friends in his life, other than those that he made his own – in the fields and in the forest. The butterfly in his hand would open its brightly coloured wings and, 'Ho!' he would gasp in amazement. The fawn would press its cold wet nose against the back of his neck and, 'Ho!' he would call out in surprise. The frog would tickle his toes in the brook and, 'Ho!' he would laugh with delight.

In his later youth, however, the chandler's boy developed an awkward manner, which became worse when he was among people. He was painfully shy, and often forgetful and clumsy. He would sometimes mumble to himself and seemed unaware of how he behaved in front of others. He rarely looked anyone in the eye and always had the feeling that he was being watched – even when he was entirely alone. The further that he travelled from home with his wares, the more terrified he became of the unknown.

People were his greatest fear. It might take as much as an hour for him to find the courage to knock on an unfamiliar door. More than once his hands trembled uncontrollably as he passed the bundle of candles to a new customer and their money spilled through his fingers. Even entering the local provisions store was a trial after he had accidentally knocked over an open sack of flour above the storekeeper's daughter, and the girl swore that she would hate him forever.

In the evenings, his father would sit by the fire and

often thought that he had been wrong to deny his son schooling. However, without his wife, who had passed away when his son was a baby, he could not have supported them both without his son's help in the workshop. Hopefully, his father assured himself, the boy would come around in time, but sometimes he thought that his son might not manage the business alone and would bring ruin upon himself. In his darker moments, he even feared for his son's future if his mind and manners got the better of him, and he failed to master himself properly.

One afternoon the boy returned early from his deliveries with blood running from his nose, his mouth split and one eye blackened. When his father questioned him, the boy refused to answer, but later in the village tavern his father discovered that a group had set about him in the road that afternoon.

'They thrashed him senseless,' said the innkeeper. 'He offered no resistance.'

For several days the boy refused to leave the house and retreated further within himself. Gradually, however, he recovered and returned to his work, but he promised himself that in future, of those who he was unsure or afraid, he would simply avoid altogether. He perfected his skills as a candle maker and learned all that his father could teach him, but still remained apart from the life of the village, except when buying supplies or selling his wares.

As his father aged before him, the young candle maker took on the business alone. To his father's surprise he improved their techniques and even reformed the workshop. News of his advancements spread beyond the district, and soon he was making candles for the homes of the wealthy and the cathedral in the great city. However, with all his achievements, the lad always had a serious expression on his face, as though he carried an enormous weight upon his shoulders. Yet, he fulfilled his duties and more besides, but now held his feelings close within him and even kept them from his own father.

Sleeping was another problem. He had once found himself alone in the forest at night, barely able to see his hand before his face, and since then he imagined misshapen images coming at him in the dark. He often had dreams that he was falling through the air from a great height to the ground, with nothing to grasp hold of or keep him aloft. Sometimes he would scream out during the night in blind terror, and so he took to working at night and resting throughout the day, although he could never properly settle as a customer might knock on the door at any time.

Nevertheless, for all his faults, if faults they were, the old chandler loved his son and remained proud of him throughout his life. He told him so on many occasions, which cheered the lad and helped his progress.

***

Every month the young candle maker, as he now was, filled his cart and pulled it over the heath to the Squire's manor. He was well known by the butlers, chambermaids and kitchen staff, and they were always pleased to see him. After the long journey and his business was completed, they would feed him in the kitchen, where fresh meat, poultry and vegetables were prepared and cooked for the manor's dining room. He never climbed the stairs to the main house and saw the splendid large rooms that his candles would light, nor did he ever meet the family who lived there and made it their home. In the last month of the year, the head cook would give him a small portion of the winter banquet to take away, and perhaps a bottle from the wine cellar for his father.

On one occasion he was returning home across the heath in the rain when he heard a voice cry out in the twilight. He looked back to the manor and then towards the village, but there was no one on the trodden path that crossed the heath. The cry came again. For a moment he thought that it might be his imagination and was about to ignore the outburst, when, in the distance, he saw a great horse standing calmly on the heath before the sunset and a man lying at its feet.

The lad thought about walking on and passing by the two shapes set against the evening sky, but then he had an awful feeling inside him that was worse than any of his fears. Cautiously, he dragged his cart towards the horse and its injured rider. He stood before the horse, which was sweating in the wet, and held it by the reins. He ran his hand along its neck, fascinated by the animal. The horse was large and powerful but did not mind his touch, and, as its scent entered his nostrils, the lad breathed in heavily and felt secure and safe.

'You know who I am?' asked the man on the ground.

The lad replied without taking his eyes off the horse.

'No, sir.'

'My leg's broken. Think my hunting days are over.'

The man watched the lad admiring his horse.

'He is lame and cannot be ridden. Will you help me?'

The lad finally turned and looked at the man lying helplessly at his feet. He was large and very heavy, too heavy to carry on his back, and so he raised the man up onto his one good leg and sat him in the handcart.

'Which way?' asked the lad.

'The manor,' replied the man, who was now making himself comfortable in the cart and opening a silver hipflask of sherry.

The lad pulled the cart over the soft ground and back onto the path, while the horse followed closely behind. They reached the top of the heath then headed down to where the path joined the road that led to the manor. The lad struggled on, pulling the cart with all his strength, sweating hard with his legs and arms aching from the work, while the Squire grew all the merrier from his sherry.

At the house the estate workers were gathered in the courtyard with lanterns, preparing to search for the missing Squire. As the lad passed through the great iron gates, he fell exhausted to his knees. The workers turned to see the Squire and his horse, and one cried out to the house.

'He is returned, ma'am.'

Immediately the Squire's family and servants spilled out the front door of the manor and ran towards them. The lad quickly got to his feet and stood nervously in the commotion, but the Squire gripped the sleeve of his jacket so that he could not run off.

'Fetch the doctor,' cried the Squire's wife.

'Never mind the doctor, I want that horse fit for next season.'

'Why, you old fool,' scolded the Squire's wife.

7

'And who's this with you?'

'Dunno,' said the Squire. 'Met him on me travels. Saved my life, he did.'

'Bless the boy,' exclaimed the Squire's wife, and she turned to the head butler.

'Take him inside. See you look after him.'

'Very good, ma'am.'

The butler nodded to the lad and they walked towards the house, while a great fuss was made of the Squire by his relatives and staff. Together they climbed the main steps of the manor and passed through the front door into the grand entrance hall.

The floor was carpeted with fine rugs. Paintings and mirrors with elegant gilt frames hung on the walls. Intricate plasterwork covered the ceiling, and from it swung glass chandeliers with candles that lit up the whole passage.

'This way,' called the butler to the lad, who had fallen behind as he admired the furniture and ornaments that decorated the hall.

The butler opened a small side door and they walked down a narrow flight of steps to a room with one tiny window. There was a bed with clean linen, a pine dressing table, a china jug and washbasin, and a wicker chair. The butler lit a candle on the dressing table.

'Do you need anything else before you retire?' the butler asked politely.

'No,' replied the lad.

'Then I'll wake you in the morning,' said the butler, and he left the room.

The lad stayed awake all night. He listened to the celebrations for the Squire's safe return in the rooms upstairs and wished that he could be part of them.

When the candle went out, he sat on the bed in the dark and watched the stars pass by the window until dawn.

In the morning the butler came for him. They ate breakfast together in the kitchen with the other servants. The Squire's groom sat at the head of the table in a furious mood.

'I told him that horse was no good on heavy soil.'

'Will the horse recover?' asked the lad nervously.

'He'll run again,' answered the groom, with his mouth stuffed full of poached egg. 'But on the firm!'

'May I see the horse?'

The groom looked up from his plate in surprise and then turned to the butler, who nodded approvingly.

As they left the kitchen, the butler whispered in the groom's ear. The groom turned thoughtfully to the lad then showed him outside into the frosty morning.

The Squire's stable was the finest in the district. Every stall was home to a champion hunter or flat racer. The lad watched in fascination as the stable hands groomed and saddled each horse before leaving for the gallops.

The groom looked on closely as the lad cautiously entered the stall of the Squire's favourite horse and again stroked it by the neck.

'Do you like horses?' asked the groom.

The lad turned to the groom and nodded to him with a broad smile across his face.

When he returned home, the lad's father met him at the door of the cottage. They went inside and the lad told him everything that had happened.

'I thought the wolves had got you,' said the old man. 'You must have had quite an adventure.'

'I'm going to learn to ride,' said the lad anxiously.

'The Squire's groom has offered me a horse. Can we spare the time?'

His father looked up in surprise but secretly overjoyed that his son had found an interest outside their home.

'Why, of course, my boy,' he replied, then slumped back into his chair by the fire. 'By all means.'

'Is anything wrong?' asked the lad.

'No, no, nothing,' answered his father earnestly. 'I've just got something in my eye, that's all.'

The lad returned to his work, but now with more energy than before and excited at the prospect that lay ahead.

The next day a stable hand from the manor arrived with a horse and saddle. Together the two lads repaired and swept out the old barn beside the cottage. On the following day the horse was saddled, and the stable hand helped the lad through his first ride before returning to the manor.

'I'll see you on Riding's Day,' joked the stable hand as he waved goodbye. The lad smiled back and nodded to his new friend, then continued grooming the horse for the next day's ride.

From then on the lad cared for the Squire's horse every moment that he could spare. Each day he rode the horse a little further from the cottage, and gradually he came to know its moods and character. Over the following months he became more confident with his riding, and he took the horse from walking to trotting across the district. In his work too there were improvements and he acquired a calmer nature, which eased his life all the more.

The lad's father was now of advanced age. He had watched his son grow from a child into a young man, and he was now certain that the lad had secured his future and would succeed in life. He knew that his son could manage the home and business in his own way. Moreover, he felt content with himself and how he had spent his years on earth. The old chandler was satisfied with all that he had done in his life, yet he now knew, without any feelings of regret or malice towards anyone, that he could do no more.

One evening the old man, at peace with himself but more tired than ever before, fell asleep in his chair by the fire and never woke.

'It was a simple service,' said the storekeeper to his wife, when he returned to his shop. 'There was just the chandler's boy and myself. He's a deep one, that lad.'

The storekeeper's daughter listened on.

'As they were filling in the grave, he turned to me and said if he was not his son, everything the old chandler knew would now be lost.

'I asked him where would that leave us, and do you know what he said?'

'In the dark.'

Two

After his father died, the young candle maker comforted himself with his work and now laboured for many more hours than he had before. At work he found that he could maintain his inner feelings by concentrating on the job before him, without dwelling too much on his sorrow. He spent all night in his workshop and only allowed himself the hour before dawn to ride. Then he would return to the cottage, stable the horse and sleep. When he woke in the mid-afternoon, he would return to work.

The villagers got to know his habits and would not disturb the candle maker until the sun was lowering in the sky. The unusual hours that he kept did no harm to the business. In fact, his working pattern had quite the opposite effect. Often people would not notice that they had run out of candles until later in the day, and then they would hurry to the candle maker's door for a new supply to see them through another night. The hours suited everyone and the business flourished.

Every month the candle maker had money to save, and after only a year there was a small fortune stored away in an iron pot beside the fire. He still made his regular deliveries to the village but rarely spoke more than a few words to anyone. His quiet and cautious manner was like a cloak that he wore to shield his true self from the outside world. He kept his life private from other people and never let anyone enter his home.

Naturally rumours of the young man, who was still widely known as the chandler's boy, spread throughout the district. Talk of his behaviour often said that there might even be something wicked about him, his secret trade and the way that he lived.

'They say he only comes out at night,' asked a traveller to the innkeeper.

'He works the night,' replied the innkeeper. 'And rests the day.'

'You don't find that a bit odd?' continued the traveller.

'Is your life so perfect?' asked the innkeeper.

The traveller drained his tankard of beer and left the inn.

***

Every morning after the night's work was completed, the candle maker would hang up his apron, fill the stable with fresh straw and saddle the horse for the dawn ride. Just the thought of once again racing across the heath eased the toil of his working life. He never covered the same ground often and usually changed the route of each ride. On horseback the unknown no longer held the same fear to the young candle maker, and eventually he knew every field and track in the district. Sometimes he would just walk beside the horse holding the reins, or they would trot along the tracks that crossed the heath. Mostly, though, they would thunder across field after field and soar over the hedgerows.

Riding was the only pleasure that the candle maker had apart from his work. He was never awkward or shy on the horse. He feared nothing in the saddle and was as much surprised by his own abilities as a rider as he was by those of the horse. They grew to trust one another. If the lad faltered, then so would the horse, but as they learned more of each other they came to believe that there was no limit to the speed they could gallop or height they could jump. They never entered the village and kept away from passers-by. Both could sense if someone was near and would quickly turn the other way.

After two years together, concealed from the world, they could race across any ground in the district as though horse and rider were one.

***

Riding's Day was in the last week of autumn. Early in the morning the villagers would gather in a field below the meadow, where long tables were set out and laid with fine linen and refreshments of meat pies and ale for the competitors. There were pony races for the children and timed events in which carts were drawn around a placed course of obstacles. In the afternoon the stable hands crossed the finishing line of the steeplechase, which had started from the manor. Everyone cheered their safe return and even more if they had the winning horse. The Squire awarded the first prize, which usually went to one of his own jockeys. However, the last event of the day was the most popular.

The Squire never entered the vault, partly because it was a test of daring between the villagers but mostly because he would not risk the life of one of his own horses, or less a jockey, in such a dangerous contest. He would not even place a bet on the favourite, as the outcome of the event was so uncertain.

The butcher's son had won the vault for the last two years running. He was a popular lad among the local girls and promised to the storekeeper's daughter, but even his talents on a horse could not draw money from the Squire.

The vault was a straight-line gallop over fences that were spaced unevenly and grew higher towards the finish. A tankard of ale was placed on the fencepost of each hurdle, and if a drop was spilled the event was lost. The competitors drew lots and the butcher's son had won the first place, which meant that he would run on the best ground before it was cut up by the horses of the other riders. He had few rivals but two other young men from the village had entered a token to compete.

The candle maker remembered the words of the stable hand, who had helped him with the horse, and now, having watched him win the steeplechase from the hill, decided that he would confront his fear of the villagers and meet him again.

He walked down to the field with the horse on its reins and pressed his way unnoticed through the crowd, which was watching the draw for the vault. The candle maker found the lad grooming his winning mount beside the course rail.

'Congratulations,' he said.

The stable hand turned around and smiled in surprise when he recognised his friend.

'I would have won last year but he threw me at the last.'

'What was your prize?'

'Three shillings.'

The two lads spoke briefly about their lives since they had parted, but the crowd's cheers for the riders in the vault eventually ended their conversation.

The butcher's son held the winning position, without having touched a fence. The first of his rivals had crashed out half way through the course and was carried from the field with his skull cracked open. The second had cleared the fences but tipped the ale from one of the posts, while his horse had broken a hoof as it made for the line.

'Foolhardy, the master calls it,' said the Squire's jockey to the candle maker. 'Not for a horseman.'

The two lads wished each other well, and the candle maker turned to leave, while the butcher's son addressed the crowd.

'Is there no one man enough to try and match me?' he asked from his saddle, after drinking a tankard of ale.

'You there!' he called out, while the candle maker climbed onto the horse. 'I say, you there.'

The candle maker rode forward nervously with the villagers closing in around him.

'Who is he?' asked the butcher's son to the steward, who could only shake his head in return.

There were murmurs in the crowd, which spread and finally broke out into wild laughter.

'Why, 'tis the chandler's boy!' answered a voice from the crowd.

'Let him away,' cried the butcher's son, disgusted that there was no one left to challenge him, and he downed another tankard of ale.

'No match for my fine fellow,' said the butcher to

the steward.

'Mark your words,' replied the steward soberly. 'He rides the Squire's horse.'

The crowd jeered menacingly at the candle maker, who looked thoughtfully down the course. He watched the villagers, who were shouting up at him, and then did something that would change his life forever.

Perhaps it was an act of youthful daring or, perhaps, after years of loneliness, he felt that he could no longer dwell in the shadows of others. Without saying a word, the candle maker, the chandler's boy, reached for his waistband, turned firmly to the race steward and threw in his marker.

The crowd gasped in disbelief but soon cheered the candle maker, if only because they had found another rival for the butcher's son.

The candle maker rode the horse calmly through the crowd towards the start of the vault. All eyes were on him now, but he did not fear the villagers and was as sure of the horse as the horse was of him. They waited patiently for the villagers to make their bets, and when the steward's flag fell they took off like a thunderbolt.

The horse's hooves barely touched the ground for an instant. They leapt over the first fence, the second and the third easily. The higher fences were tougher, as the horse had to alter its footing on the uneven ground, yet they cleared the last fence, the highest of all, with room to spare and not a drop of ale from any tankard was spilled.

The candle maker raced past the butcher's son and the storekeeper's daughter, who were watching from the rail, and when they crossed the finishing line the crowd went mad.

Most of the villagers cheered the candle maker for

completing the vault and putting the butcher's son in his place. Some, however, shouted with rage, as they had lost their bets, while others fought in the mud over their money. Yet the Squire, watching from his chair on the winning stand, simply rose to his feet in amazement, removed his three-cornered hat and looked for his prize jockey, who nodded to him with approval.

The Squire climbed down from the winning stand and cautiously approached the candle maker as he dismounted the horse.

'You proved me wrong about this one,' said the Squire, patting the horse on the neck. 'I never had any faith in him. Perhaps that was the trouble.'

'He's still your horse, sir,' replied the candle maker, but the Squire shook his head.

'He'd never ride like that for any of my men.'

Meanwhile, the steward was trying to calm the villagers.

'There is no separating them,' he cried out. 'It is an even draw. We shall split the money between sides.'

'There is one test that remains,' said the Squire, turning to the steward. Suddenly the steward's eyes widened, and he quickly pulled a hunting horn from his belt to signal the squabbling villagers.

The Devil's Ditch was sixteen yards of still water with low banks on either side that no one in living memory had cleared on horseback, except for the Squire's father and he had tumbled on landing.

The Squire called out to the butcher's son, 'Do you accept the challenge, lad?'

'I do, sir.'

The butcher, however, was against the idea and spoke quietly to the Squire.

'The boy is young and foolish. I urge you, sir, do not indulge him.'

However, the villagers were already running down the hill towards the ditch, where they pushed each other aside for the best positions. They gathered along the banks on either side but left a space in the middle for the riders. The butcher's son and the candle maker rode down together, with the Squire, the steward and the butcher leading the way.

When they reached the ditch, the candle maker and the butcher's son dismounted and stood before the steward, who was calling for order among the excited villagers. Yet the candle maker did not hear him speak. As he walked slowly forward to stare out over the vast ditch, he thought it impossible that anyone could leap a horse over such a large stretch of water. His fear of people returned and he spoke nervously to the Squire.

'I can't jump that.'

After a moment's thought the Squire replied, 'I've seen you ride. I believe you can.'

'No, sir,' returned the candle maker, shaking his head. 'Not that.'

'You doubt yourself?' asked the Squire firmly. 'You don't believe in yourself? Well, I believe in you.' Then he called out to the butcher, who was now arguing with his son, 'And I've a hundred guineas to prove it!'

The villagers all cheered, and they cheered again even louder when the butcher finally matched the Squire's wager.

'Who will call?' asked the steward, and the butcher's son nodded to the candle maker.

'Tops or tails?' called the steward, and he threw a coin into the air.

'Tails,' said the candle maker.

The steward carefully looked down at the coin that now lay at his feet.

'Tops!' he cried, and the candle maker again felt that the task before him was too great.

'Do not think of the distance to jump,' said the Squire to the candle maker. 'Think only of where you shall land and you will succeed.'

This raised his mood a little, and when the candle maker was back in the saddle the ditch did not seem as wide as it had first appeared. Then he recognised the storekeeper's daughter, who was smiling at him from the crowd, and, to him, the ditch shrunk even more. As he smiled back at her, the butcher's son rode up in front of him.

'You've a bold spirit, chandler, to think you can better me.'

The butcher's son sneered angrily at the candle maker, then he took a whip to his horse and they galloped off back up the hill.

When he reached the top, he whipped the horse once more and they thundered down towards the ditch with the crowd cheering them all the way. The butcher's son rode like a madman, whipping the horse again and again, and with each stroke the horse ran faster in pain and fear. As they neared the ditch, the butcher's son was filled with rage, but the horse was now terrified and reared at the bank, throwing its rider onto the muddy ground.

The storekeeper's daughter ran forward from the crowd, which was shouting in anger or laughing in surprise and delight at the butcher's son. She tried to help him to his feet, but he struck her across the face and left her lying on the bank, then he walked off the field with the crowd in uproar behind him.

The storekeeper's daughter stood up shaken and confused. She wiped her bleeding mouth with the back of her hand and then made her way towards the candle maker, who dismounted from the horse to meet her.

'Are you alright?' he asked.

She nodded to him, unable to speak for a moment, while the tears dried on her face. They stood looking into each other's eyes, somehow unable to remove their gaze. The storekeeper's daughter and the candle maker were not at all alike. She was much taller than him, a few years older and darker in hair and skin, and yet they seemed strangely drawn together. They recognised each other from the past, but the passage of time on their characters seemed to be responsible for the attraction that was now present between them. Furthermore, their childhood disagreement over a bag of flour, like the noise of the crowd around them, simply faded away into the background.

Then the steward approached, having calmed the villagers for a second time.

'Well?' he asked sternly. 'Are you going to stand there all day or show us what you're made of?'

The candle maker was still unsure and spoke anxiously to the storekeeper's daughter.

'Do you believe I can cross that?'

She thought seriously for a moment, with her mouth screwed to one side, and then replied smiling, 'Why not?'

Suddenly something rushed through the candle maker's body as though he had just passed through a barrier between darkness and light. He felt again like the child that he had been, but now grown into a man who was no longer afraid of the world and its people.

21

There was no doubt in his mind about himself, and he saw a future of possibilities and all that he could accomplish in life. The weight that he had carried on his shoulders was lifted. His awkwardness, shyness and fear had vanished, and he climbed back onto the horse with his head dizzy from the new experience.

He looked down at the storekeeper's daughter, who was still smiling up at him.

'I believe,' she whispered, and another rush of excitement raced through his body.

'Ho, ho!' cried the candle maker, and swiftly he and the horse set off up the hill again.

The horse galloped towards the ditch at a ferocious speed that none of the villagers had ever seen before. The candle maker fixed his eyes on the opposite bank, the horse leapt forward and, in no time at all, they were there.

Three

The candle maker rode the horse back to the village surrounded by people cheering him. The Squire held the horse's reins in one hand and his tankard of ale in the other, while smiling broadly at the thought of his winnings. His jockey walked beside, looking up at his friend and quietly admiring what he had achieved. The steward trotted along nearby, clapping the horse on its hindquarters and puffing with enjoyment as he tried to keep up with the others. Spread out beside them and to the rear, the whole village was shouting and applauding the candle maker, who was now quite overwhelmed by the attention that he was receiving. Then the storekeeper's daughter pushed her way through the villagers and grabbed his arm. The candle maker looked down, and when he saw her face again, smiling at him as before, he instantly bent down to lift her up by the waist and sat her on the horse in front of him. The villagers cheered again, and the Squire raised his tankard to the candle maker and the storekeeper's daughter, and then he took another mouthful of ale. The whole procession marched triumphantly into the village. When they reached the inn the Squire stood on an old tree stump and steadied himself with the steward's shoulder, as he proudly addressed the assembled villagers.

'My friends!' he called out. 'We will not forget this day for many a year. What this young man has done has touched our hearts and raised our spirits. Let us remember his triumph and rejoice.' Cheers rang out from the villagers.

'Rejoice in his success today,' continued the Squire, after he had again refreshed himself with his ale. 'And keep it in mind for others who come after. Tell them the tale of the young candle maker, and tell them you saw him with your own eyes. He did it, indeed. By Jove, he did it!'

Again there were cheers from the villagers, and the Squire became so overcome by the moment that he burst into a display of unrestrained merriment.

'Ha, ha!' he called out, with tears in his eyes, then, 'Whoops!' he cried as his feet slipped off the tree stump and he fell backwards into the horse trough.

The villagers were silenced, and the candle maker leapt from the horse to find the Squire, who had now completely disappeared below the water. However, everyone soon roared with pleasure as the Squire rose from the trough still holding his tankard and booming with laughter. He embraced the candle maker as though he was his son and spoke fondly to him.

'Well done, my boy. I never thought I'd live to see the day. It was like seeing my own father again. You've made me so happy.'

The Squire was helped into the inn, where there followed music, singing and dancing. There was good food and drink for everyone, and the candle maker was introduced to all the villagers. He ate with the storekeeper and danced with his daughter, and the more the evening wore on, the more he felt that he was again part of a loving family.

Outside the inn the candle maker waved goodbye to the villagers and walked up the hill to his cottage. He lay comfortably on his bed and slept peacefully the whole night through. He only woke in the morning, when the sun was high in the sky and he heard someone knocking at the door. For a moment his fear of people returned, but it soon vanished when he saw the storekeeper's daughter standing beside the saddled horse and smiling towards him in the morning sunlight.

'You left him tied to the inn last night,' she said wryly.

'Did I?' replied the candle maker, rubbing his forehead. 'I don't remember.'

'He's very annoyed with you,' she continued. 'He says he wants to live with me from now on.'

'Can you ride?' asked the candle maker.

'I'll find someone to teach me. You wouldn't know of anyone, would you?'

'Perhaps,' said the candle maker, and he walked towards her.

'Haven't you forgotten something?' she asked knowingly.

The candle maker thought for a moment, grumbled to himself and then returned to the cottage, as he realised that he was dressed in only his nightshirt.

The horse carried the storekeeper's daughter and the candle maker over hills, through valleys and across streams. They held their arms around each other and hands clasped firmly together.

They did not care how far they travelled or for how long, yet they felt the comfort of each other's company and the sun shining on their faces, while golden leaves fell all around them. The horse took them deep into the forest and only halted in a clearing beside the trickling brook, where flowers bloomed on the forest floor and birds sang from the trees.

'Where are we?' asked the storekeeper's daughter, as the candle maker helped her down from the horse.

'I used to play here as a child,' he replied and turned slyly to the horse. 'I thought I was the only one who knew of this place.' Then he paused thoughtfully. 'I often wished I could share it with someone.'

'It's beautiful.'

'Yes, it is,' agreed the candle maker, and they smiled to each other – overwhelmed with happiness.

***

When they returned to the village, the storekeeper and his wife were waiting for them.

The storekeeper's daughter raced to her mother and they fled excitedly into the kitchen, whispering frantically. The storekeeper led the candle maker into the front room, where they shared a jug of port wine. Then the storekeeper filled the bowls of two long-steamed clay pipes with tobacco.

'Would you care for some?' said the storekeeper, and he passed a pipe to the candle maker.

'Thank you,' replied the candle maker out of politeness, but he broke out into a sudden coughing fit as the pipe was lighted and he took his first puff of smoke.

When the candle maker had recovered, the two men sat comfortably back in their wicker chairs, drinking and smoking, and talked the rest of the day through. By the evening they knew each other as well as father and son, and over dinner the storekeeper's wife came to know the candle maker as though he was her own child. They raised their glasses in good cheer to one another and blessed their future lives together.

From then on the storekeeper's daughter visited the candle maker's cottage most mornings. They would spend the day preparing a home for themselves and each evening she returned to her family, more certain that she had chosen the right man for a husband. On other days the candle maker visited her in the village, where he found that people now viewed him in quite a different way. The villagers were genuinely pleased to see him and his future wife together, and waved approvingly to the young couple as they walked by.

At their wedding in the little village church, the storekeeper's wife cried throughout the entire ceremony. Half the village turned out in their Sunday clothes to see the storekeeper pass his daughter's hand to the candle maker, while the Squire's jockey stood by his side and handed him a gold ring for her finger. The couple were then pronounced married and, as the church pipe organ rang out, the candle maker lifted his bride's veil and kissed her tenderly on the lips.

That evening the guests assembled at the inn, where a long table was prepared for dinner. The candle maker and his wife welcomed everyone at the door, and many handed them gifts as they arrived. The storekeeper presented the candle maker with a pair of shiny black leather riding boots, while his wife gave her daughter a long red winter coat with white fur trim and little gold bells for buttons. After the meal, music filled the room, and the candle maker and his wife swept across the floor in each other's arms, watched in wonder by everyone around them, but as though they were the only two people in the world.

In the morning the candle maker woke to find sunlight lying softly across his wife's face. No dreams had come to him during the hours of darkness, and again, for only the second time since he was a child, he had slept the night through.

Marriage transformed the life of the candle maker. He no longer worked all night, but he and his wife still kept the cottage door unlatched until late in the evening, while a light shone in the window to welcome any customer who might call. They spent almost every moment of the day together, either in the cottage or out delivering their wares.

The candle maker's wife taught him to cook on the old pot-bellied stove, which had not been lit since his father died, while she became equally at home in the workshop, where she helped her husband draw out wax on flaxen wicks and hang them by the dozen on the iron ceiling hooks. She also mixed dyes from bluebells, violets and rose petals, and added them to the melted wax to make coloured candles for children's bedsides. She patched the worn knees and elbows of her husband's clothes and darned the holes in his socks. She tidied the garden, and planted herbs and fruit bushes around the cottage, while the candle maker found that he could produce a day's stock of candles in half the time and with less effort than it had ever taking him before. A day, it seemed, went by in a second, and yet appeared to last forever.

Together the candle maker and his wife gave each other the most precious gift that anyone could ever hope to receive in life. They had time to gaze into each other's eyes in the morning. Time to walk in the afternoon sunlight. Time to sit quietly together or talk for hours beside the fire in the evening. Time to visit their relations, the many friends that they made and the children of the village, who would race towards the candle maker and his wife with their arms outstretched to greet them. They always gave small treats to the children, and filled their hands with fruit or ginger biscuits from their garden and kitchen.

'Good for business,' said the candle maker's wife to her husband, while she handed out the last of the strawberries, and he nodded back to her in mock agreement.

The candle maker was often surprised by how easily his wife took to their new life together, and he too surprised himself by what he could achieve in a single day with her by his side. They threw themselves into the life of the village, and took part in all its yearly customs and traditions. Every week the candle maker's wife visited the homes where there was illness, and brought hot broth and comfort to the sick. Together they called on the elderly, infirm and alone, and sat with them for hours, listening to the tales of their lives and their happiest times. When May approached, they helped prepare the village green for the annual fair. They decorated the maypole with the children, and dressed the village well with spring flowers. At the end of summer they helped gather the crops from the fields and gave thanks with the farmers at the harvest festival.

On cold winter nights they would take candles to every home in the village and leave them on the windowsills, while they waved to the families inside through the frosted glass. When they returned to the cottage, the candle maker would stamp the snow from his black leather riding boots, and his wife would hang her long red winter coat, with white fur trim and little gold bells for buttons, behind the door. Then they would sit together, warm and content by the fire, and toast their good fortune with a glass of their homemade mulled wine.

***

After three years of married life together, the candle maker's wife told her husband that she was expecting a baby. The child would be born in the middle of the coming winter, and they spent the following months preparing the cottage for the new arrival. They placed a cot with warm blankets and embroidered pillows by their bedside. The candle maker thought that the child would be a boy, and so he carved a toy soldier from wood and painted its uniform. His wife, however, favoured a girl, and she spent the evenings sitting in her chair and sewing a soft doll from coloured rags. Then they sat the gifts above the fire contentedly and waited for the baby.

As the time grew near, the candle maker's wife became weaker from the child that she was carrying, but she always remained cheerful in front of her husband. Her mother often visited to help care for her daughter, and each time she always brought more provisions for child. Meanwhile, the candle maker stayed awake night after night to comfort his wife and attend to her, even though she kept telling him that it was unnecessary and he would do better to rest his head.

On the shortest day of the year, the candle maker's wife began to feel the first pains of childbirth. Her mother brought the Squire's doctor through the snow to the cottage, and he told the candle maker to wait by the fire, while he nursed his wife throughout the day and late into the night. The candle maker sat patiently in his chair, knowing that he could do nothing for his wife, and could only listen helplessly as her cries filled the cottage.

In the morning the doctor woke the candle maker, who had at last fallen asleep in his chair by the fire.

'I'm very sorry,' said the doctor, with the most solemn expression on his face. 'The child died in the mother. I could save neither.'

The candle maker trembled with fear.

'No!' he exclaimed. 'I don't believe you.'

The doctor took him by the arm and led the candle maker to the rear of the cottage, where his wife was lying peacefully on their bed. Her mother was on her knees sobbing beside her departed daughter. For a moment the candle maker thought that he could wake his wife from her condition, but when he held her hand he realised the truth, as it was cold as the frost outside.

In the afternoon the storekeeper arrived with a horse and cart, and the candle maker's wife was taken from the cottage in a wooden casket. The storekeeper touched the candle maker on the shoulder as he was leaving, but he could not find a word to say and so left him staring blankly towards the dying embers of the fire.

As the doctor made his way to the door, the candle maker suddenly turned to him and spoke.

'The baby, you say.' Then he paused thoughtfully for a moment. 'Never saw the light?'

The doctor shook his head and left the candle maker with his thoughts, sitting alone by the smouldering fire.

Four

That night a terrible cry was heard in the village. It came from up the hill, on the edge of the forest, where the candle maker lived. The villagers ran to their homes in fear that a wild animal was loose, or perhaps a demon from another world had come for their souls. The screams rang out all night, churning the blood in everyone who heard them, as the candle maker flew into a violent rage. He threw himself around the cottage and beat his face with his fists. He smashed furniture to splinters, tore the coat from his back and cast it on the fire. In the stable the horse panicked and was so afraid that it kicked down the door, then fled in blind terror and never returned.

The candle maker roared with anger. He damned the world and every living creature in it. He drank the last of the mulled wine and smashed the bottle on the burning logs. Then he threw the broken sticks of furniture onto the fire and collapsed in front of the roaring blaze, with his back to the door and his eyes boiling with fury.

In the morning the storekeeper made his way through the snow to the cottage and knocked at the door. There was smoke billowing from the chimney but no one answered his calls. The next day he brought his wife and they tried for an hour to raise the candle maker, but the door remained locked solid and the windows were firmly bolted from the inside. All they could see through the glass was a dark shape nodding before the fire.

After a week the storekeeper and his wife stopped trying to draw the candle maker out of his misery. After a few months no one from the village dared go near the cottage, in fear of hearing the few words that were ever heard from within.

'Be gone!'

In time, most of the villagers accepted the life this strange man had chosen for himself, again apart from them and alone. Some cursed him for having to travel several miles to the next village to find a chandler, while others blamed him for their every misfortune. Only the local children were brave enough to venture close to his cottage and throw stones at the door. However, no matter how much they tormented him, the door never opened, while inside the man grew old ahead of his years.

Mostly he sat by the fire, drinking his mulled wine and muttering angrily to the flames. His food came from the forest, which provided him with all that he needed, wood for the fire and food for his belly. Occasionally, shortly after nightfall, a dark shape was seen foraging about on the forest floor or chasing wildfowl through the trees, but no one ever saw its face.

The man grew fat about the middle. His nose and cheeks turned red as cherries. His beard grew long and full, and with it his hair turned white with age, and still the cottage door never opened to another living soul.

Life became harsher for the villagers. The candle maker and his wife seemed to have taken with them some part of the village, and now each dwelling had an unwelcoming appearance. The villagers soon let the months of the year pass without their yearly celebrations and festivals to mark them.

Some years the crops failed. Livestock perished and people grew thin with hunger. Few travellers ever stayed more than a night at the inn before hurriedly continuing on their journey. Illness often swept through the village, and during the outbreaks few people would open their doors to their neighbour and risk catching some deadly infection. The road through its middle fell into ruin and woods grew untended around the village, which rapidly became lost to the world. However, life carried on through the hardships – if life it could be called.

***

Twenty winters past. Each seemed worse than the one before, colder, darker and longer. Some villagers never saw them out and lay in their homes until they were found in the spring. Their houses were never occupied again. The roofs fell in and their walls collapsed around them. Wild flowers and creepers quickly took over the plot, and after a year or so no one could tell if the place had ever been lived in before.

People grew old quickly. The young worked the land without the direction of their elders, who were too frail to labour, and children were forced to help their parents at home, rather than attend the village school, which eventually closed. Childhood was brief, and daily chores replaced games and playtime.

Winter seemed to come earlier each year. Some

villagers were often unprepared for the season, while others were caught out by the first fall of snow. A boy and his sister were gathering firewood at the edge of the forest when the huge flakes began dropping gently around them. They held out their hands, then closed their eyes and caught them on their tongues, where they melted into freezing water that dribbled down their cheeks. They made shapes in the snow and threw handfuls at each other, until their world was changed completely and darkness came upon them.

The path that they had walked was gone, and now there were no familiar sights to guide them home. The boy clung to his sister's hand and unknowingly led her, cold and wet, away from the village, then, tired himself, let it slip deep in the forest. After only a few steps without her by his side, she was gone.

The boy cried out for his sister in the dark, but the snow dulled his voice and no answer returned. In panic he ran blind through the forest with his arms outstretched, but hit his head on the low bow of a tree and was knocked out cold.

Several minutes past. The boy lay in darkness, unconscious on the forest floor with snow quickly covering his face. Just the faintest light, a tiny speck, like a single star in the night sky, shone towards him through the branches. The star's light struck the corner of the boy's eye, which might have remained closed for all time, and it opened.

The boy sat up against the base of a tree, shivering and gazing numbly at the distant yellow glow. Somehow he found the strength to stand and pushed himself towards its source. Gradually, the spot grew into a circle of brightness that lit his face and warmed him inside. He walked on, stumbling through the snow and out of the forest, where the light slowly formed into the window of a cottage.

Snow was piled high on the window ledge, but the boy brushed it clear and stared through the frosted glass. He tapped on the window and cried out in despair. Something was moving inside but it would not answer his calls. He hit the window with his fist, and again until he broke the glass and cut his hand. Then a hollow voice called out from inside the cottage.

'What do you want of me?'

'Help, sir,' replied the boy.

'Help yourself!' returned the voice.

'Not for me,' said the boy, 'for my sister. She is lost.'

'I can do nothing for you,' came the voice again.

'She is lost, I say. Please,' the boy pleaded, 'believe me.'

There was no answer.

The boy stood back helplessly from the cottage, but he would not give up and so shouted again, louder this time, in desperation and anger at the broken window.

'Believe me!'

Again there was silence. The boy moved to the front of the cottage, where he listened at the door. After a moment he turned to walk away, but then a bolt was thrown from within and the door slowly creaked open.

The boy looked inside. He cautiously stepped over the threshold and found the shell of a man standing before a great fire. The man turned slowly to face the boy. His face was burnt red by the fire, his beard was full and his white hair fell down upon his shoulders. He looked at the boy and noticed his injured hand, then took a cloth from his waistband, which the boy wrapped around the cut to stop the bleeding.

'My sister, sir. She is lost in the forest.'

'I cannot leave this house,' said the man firmly.

'She is alone in the dark and snow.'

'Not tonight!' insisted the man. 'Of all nights.' Then he saw that the boy was close to tears. 'I'll give you a light. *You* can look for her.'

The man went to the rear of the cottage and returned with a glass lantern. The boy watched as the man carefully primed it with wax and lit the wick with a spill from the fire. Suddenly the whole room exploded into light.

'Bright enough for you?' asked the man.

The boy carried the lantern to the door and then turned again to the man.

'Won't you help me?' asked the boy. 'She will die in the cold.'

'I have nothing to wear in this weather,' said the man. 'I'd freeze to death myself out there.'

The boy nodded towards the door, where there hung a long red winter coat with white fur trim and little gold bells for buttons.

The man spun around to face the boy.

'No!'

'Please,' begged the boy. 'There is no one else.'

The man thought for a moment. He could see that the boy was right and without his help his sister would surely perish in the snow.

Nervously, the man approached the door and lifted the coat from its hook. The boy watched as he stroked the white fur knowingly. The man turned slyly back to the boy, but eventually he slung the coat around his shoulders and lifted the hood over his head. Next, the man walked towards the door, where he pulled on a pair of black leather riding boots. Then he fastened the lantern to a long pole and set out into the night with the boy pulling at his hand.

Inside the huge ball of light that surrounded them, they tracked the boy's steps back to where he had fallen, then further on to where his sister lay almost covered in snow. The man lifted the child in his arms and carried her back to the cottage with the boy in front lighting their way.

When they were inside, the man wrapped the girl in blankets and sat her by the fire. Her eyes opened briefly, if only to tell her brother that she was still alive, then closed again as she fell, warm and safe, into a deep sleep.

As she slept, the man sat by the fire and poured himself a glass of mulled wine, while the boy eyed a plate of cold meat on the hearth.

'I'm very hungry, sir,' said the boy.

'The last of the roast turkey,' said the man, and he rose from his seat and passed a large slice to the boy. 'I'll make a broth for your sister.'

The boy then turned to the toy soldier and the rag doll that were sitting on the mantle shelf above the fire.

'What are those?' he asked between mouthfuls.

The man paused thoughtfully for a moment.

'They were made for someone many years ago,' said the man, and he scraped the meat into a pot on the stove.

'Didn't they want them?' asked the boy.

'They never came for them.'

'I knew you would help me,' said the boy. 'I saw the light in the window and I knew you'd help.'

'You could have knocked on any door where there

was a light in the window. Why mine?' asked the man.

'There aren't any,' said the boy, and he lit a candle from the fire and gazed into its flame.

'You don't have candles?' asked the man.

'We can't afford them,' replied the boy, still fascinated by the light before him. 'It gives you a sort of strength, doesn't it? Strength to carry on.'

'Strength?' asked the man, who was quite puzzled by the boy's suggestion. 'What sort of strength?'

'Hope, sir,' said the boy smiling.

The man grumbled to himself and returned to stirring the pot.

When she woke, the man fed the boy's sister with the broth, and all three sat quietly together beside the fire until the children were strong enough to travel.

Late in the evening the man again put on his wife's fur winter coat, lit the lantern and took the children through the snow and down the muddy lane to the village. As they approached the houses, the man slowed his step at the sight of the ruined and overgrown buildings.

'I used to know this place,' said the man, as he gazed numbly around the remains of the village. 'But not anymore.' He began shivering with fear and looked down at the boy and his sister.

'Is this my doing?' he asked, but the children did not understand him. Instead they pulled him on unwillingly towards their home, where their parents welcomed them at the door, overjoyed that they had not been lost to the season. They thanked the stranger, who had returned them safely and invited him inside their cottage, but he excused himself and drew back from their company.

Meanwhile, other villagers appeared cautiously at

their doors or windows to see the colourful figure who had suddenly appeared among them in a great ball of brightness that lit up the snowy cottages. Nervously, he watched the poor frightened souls whisper to each other. There was not one that he recognised from his past. They were all painfully thin, dirty and dressed in no more than rags. They had a dark empty look in their eyes, as though what spirit they once had in them had been snubbed out long ago. Some, however, particularly the young, were drawn towards him and brave enough to leave their homes for a closer look at the stranger. They surrounded him and smiled when they saw his large red face almost hidden behind his flowing white hair and beard. They pulled at the long red winter coat to hear the little gold bells ring.

Awkwardly, the stranger handed a bundle of candles to the children's father and was about to leave when he suddenly remembered something and turned to the boy and his sister. Slowly, he reached into the pockets of the coat and finally pulled out the toy soldier and the rag doll, and he gave them to the children. Then he lifted the hood of the coat over his head, picked up the lantern and walked away into the night, while the people returned to their homes and the village again faded into darkness.

Five

The morning after every home in the village woke to find a small bundle of candles outside the door. No one had seen him, but some of the villagers said that they had heard the stranger while they were lying in their beds, and when they saw the gifts on the doorstep knew that he must have returned during the night.

That evening the village was transformed. Faint flickers of light once again shone out from the cottage windows. Families sat together with the tiny flames burning in their homes. Children played late into the night, while their parents watched over them without fear of the darkness outside. Meanwhile, the candle maker sat quietly by his fire. He supped his mulled wine and puffed away on his clay pipe, while smiling contentedly with a warm feeling inside him.

The next day he entered the workshop, and looked around the dusty pots and moulds that had not been touched for years. He smiled when he saw his father's tools still hanging on the wall, then he sat at his cluttered bench and shrugged off the reflection of the overweight untidy man in the glass jar beside him.

The candle maker felt comfortable again at his place of work, but his heart sank when his eyes fell on a pile of dried rose petals. He tried to pick them up but they crumbled into dust that fell through his fingers, and a new feeling came over him, something that he had never experienced before in his life. It was as though he had been holding some dark dreadful secret inside him that was about to be let out. For years the secret had shielded him, not only from the world but also himself. It was as familiar to him as his own body, and yet his mind had never admitted the existence of what he held captive. He did not want to let it go but knew that he could not hold the secret inside any longer. As it left him, the candle maker slowly rested his head on his folded arms before him and wept.

He cried for his father, and his wife and the child he never saw. He cried for the villagers and himself and what he had become. He cried for the years that he had spent living alone with nothing but anger to guard himself from the world outside.

The candle maker sat up shuddering with tears pouring down his face. He tried to dry his eyes and shake himself out of his despair, but the feeling would not leave him. He sobbed hopelessly and now trembled with fear as he looked about the disused workshop. Nothing, he felt, could put things right. He thought about how he would spend the rest of his life. He could not change the past and knew that it would always be with him. He shouted out for someone to help him, but no one heard his cries.

It seemed that only he could end his misery. He turned and saw a knife beside him. In desperation he reached for it, but something had stuck it fast to the bench. He swept aside the clutter and saw layer after layer of wax set hard on its surface. Then the candle maker suddenly calmed.

He gazed through his watery eyes at the spread of

wax before him. Each layer was a season's work and there were many, one on top of the other, and all slightly different in texture and colour. Some were spread out smooth and thin, while others were thick and rough on the surface. As he looked at the wax, shapes and colours appeared before him that he thought he recognised. From where he sat they seemed tiny and of little importance, but he knew that they were everything in his life. His tears had fallen into a small gully in the wax and now slowly trickled their way along the bench. Surely, thought the candle maker, there was the brook in the forest where he had played as a child. Beside it was the road that ran through the village. There was the common and the heath. He saw the whole district set out miniature as though he were looking at the landscape from high above. He cleared more of the bench and ran his fingers over the rises and falls, as if they were passing swiftly over the hills and valleys of the outlying countryside. He found more villages, towns and the great city where he had never been, all twinkling with little specks of light from the sun that was shining in through the window. At the edge of the wax he saw the coast and, beyond it, islands in the channel, and then the shore of another land. The sun lit up the whole scene so brightly that it was as though the light was coming from the wax itself. The candle maker had to shield his eyes from the sight, but when the sun faded and he opened them again he saw that the landscape had gone and all that was left was just layers of wax on the bench.

The candle maker pulled off a piece of the wax and softened it in the warmth of his hands. He squeezed and turned the wax and made it into a ball, then he held it up before him. The light from the window shone on one side of the ball, while the other was in darkness, and the candle maker felt that he had the whole world at his fingertips. Now he knew what was to be done.

The cottage held many memories that made him sad but still feel safe from the outside world. He doubted that he could open the workshop alone but then thought of the villagers and how desperate they had become. He knew that it would be difficult to face them again, but felt that he owed them that much for his desertion and vowed to make good on the debt. He would start again, the candle maker decided. He would work the year and each winter provide enough candles for the whole village. They would have light again in their lives, he promised himself, and, with it, as the boy had said, he would give them hope.

***

For the rest of the winter the candle maker tidied the workshop. In early spring, he filled his pockets with money from the iron pot beside the fire and toured the district in search of all the materials that he would need for the coming year. He visited the nearby farms and asked if they could spare any flax for his wicks. At one the farmer's wife told him that he could pull as much as he liked, as the field had not been harvested the year before and they did not intend to plant the crop again.

On his return home he crossed the heath with a great sack on his shoulders. He stumbled on the wet ground and sat for a moment, wondering how he could move the load to his cottage before dark. As he stared out hopelessly across the heath, he saw a line of dark shapes moving along the road below. He lifted the sack and walked down to the road, where he stood before a procession of heavily loaded carts and caravans pulled by horses. They were driven by a people that he did not know, and behind them came wild animals in cages and strange beasts that he had never seen before. One of the drivers held up his hand when he saw the candle maker and halted the procession. He got down from the cart and gave the order to make camp for the night, then he turned to the candle maker. The two men were about the same age and build, yet the driver had darker skin, long black hair and a thin moustache that fell down past his chin. He wore a wide-rimmed black hat and cape. The man introduced himself and said that he was the ringmaster of a travelling circus, which was on its way to perform in the great city. The candle maker found the man strangely appealing, perhaps because they were similar but also because they were so very different. It was as though he was looking at the opposite reflection of himself in a mirror. He told the ringmaster his trade and that he needed some way to transport his wares back home.

'I've the very thing for you,' said the ringmaster, and he called for an old horse and a brightly coloured cart that he wanted to sell to be brought forward.

'He's still got a few good years left in him.'

The candle maker looked over the horse. It was not the finest animal that he had ever seen, but the horse and cart suited his purpose and a deal was struck between the two men.

'You'd best camp with us tonight,' said the ringmaster, and he invited the candle maker to join him for supper.

When the caravan was stationed and the tents raised, the candle maker and the ringmaster sat before a fire and talked, while they ate from a spit of cooked meat and drank from jars of ale. The circus musicians filled the night air with music. There was dancing by the performers, juggling with flaming clubs, tests of strength and stilt walking, while a group of tiny people argued among themselves and playfully hit each other with their hats.

'These are my people,' said the ringmaster proudly. 'I have found them from across the known world and beyond. They are vagabonds, ruffians, thieves and tricksters, every man Jack o' them. No good to anyone. No good to themselves until I came along, yet each has a gift for our show. It's the same for everyone, I suppose, but who has need of clowns and acrobats outside the circus?'

The ringmaster paused briefly and turned cautiously to the candle maker. 'I know a good thing when I see it,' he continued. 'I'm sure that you have some talent we could use.'

The candle maker sighed longingly and thought for a moment. Then he took a burnt stick that was still smoking from the fire and blew on it with one long breath. The ashes glowed, sparks flew and suddenly the stick burst into a flame that lit up his bearded face and made his eyes glisten. He did not move an inch, but the ringmaster fell back on his seat in surprise and shielded his eyes from the glare. Others too turned to see what had suddenly brightened up the campsite.

'Perhaps you would join us?' asked the ringmaster, after he had recovered and returned to his seat.

'I can't,' said the candle maker regrettably, as he

felt that he had found a like-minded fellow with whom he could share his thoughts. 'I have so very much to do here.'

'Make sure it's with that,' said the ringmaster, pointing to the burning stick.

'It is,' replied the candle maker. 'Although I'm not sure how.'

'Yes,' agreed the ringmaster. 'It's not easy to find a new place in life when youth has past us by.'

The candle maker looked at him as though he was asking for some advice. Then the ringmaster turned to him and spoke firmly.

'My business is performance. Those who come to see us want to witness something remarkable, something unique, something extraordinary that will make them forget their troubles, if only for a short time. They want something in which they can believe, and it is their belief in our abilities that makes our success all the easier. Without their trust in us we might fail, and certainly not soar to the heights that we have so far travelled, less those that we have yet to reach. Practice your art, make mistakes, polish *your* performance then show it to the world.'

'I fear they will pass me by,' said the candle maker.

'Here,' replied the ringmaster, and he handed over a heavy black bag from the stash of possessions that surrounded him. 'This should get their attention.'

The candle maker looked inside the bag and smiled broadly. He quietly thanked the ringmaster but was still unsure of his chosen mission.

'And if they mock me?'

'Nothing good ever came into this world that was not laughed at to begin with. You will find some set their minds against you, but remember if you win the

47

hearts of only a few, you can ride on that faith to the moon and back – forever.'

The candle maker looked up to the night sky and the vast bowl of stars that shone above him. He sighed again as he thought that the task he had set himself was too great for one man.

'What is it you're looking for?' asked the ringmaster.

'I want to race against the sunrise,' said the candle maker.

'Well, it's always night somewhere,' replied the ringmaster, as he made a bed for himself by the fire.

'Yes it is, isn't it?' said the candle maker thoughtfully, and a new idea began forming in his head.

'But I don't know of anything that moves that fast,' continued the ringmaster. 'A ghost, perhaps.'

'A ghost, yes. Or a spirit!' replied the candle maker, and he turned excitedly to the ringmaster, but he was already sound asleep.

The candle maker smiled to himself. He sat by the fire for the rest of the night, peacefully under the stars, with a great plan set in his mind.

***

In the morning the candle maker returned home with the horse and cart. As he neared the cottage, he saw the boy who he had helped that winter. Only a few months had past since then, but the boy had grown and was now looking for work. The candle maker was reluctant to take him on, but the boy was keen to learn, and the candle maker knew that he could not run the workshop by himself.

'Return at sunset,' said the candle maker. 'We work at night.'

The boy did as he was told, and together they prepared the materials that they would use in the coming season. Over the next few months the candle maker taught the boy his trade. He was quick to learn, and it pleased the candle maker to teach him and pass on his knowledge. Each morning after the night's work was finished, the boy returned home with a candle for his family and a little money in his pocket.

As winter approached, they worked harder and for longer hours, but still could only produce a few candles in a night. The candle maker grew more frustrated with their progress, especially when he remembered what he had achieved in the past, when he was a younger man. Sometimes he would forget where he had left one of his tools, or even what he was supposed to be doing, but the boy would simply tell him to rest by the fire in the cottage and then carried on working by himself. At the end of the season, however, the candle maker was pleased with what they had accomplished together and asked the boy if he would help him again in the spring.

'We'll make twice as many next year,' said the boy, as they counted the bundles of candles and piled them in the corner of the workshop.

'I believe so,' replied the candle maker.

A few days later, on the longest night of the year, the candle maker entered the stable and loaded the cart with bundles of candles. He harnessed the horse and tied a lantern on a pole at the front. Then he returned to the cottage, where he stood in his black leather riding boots before the long red winter coat that was hanging behind the door. He gently stroked the white

49

fur trim around the hood and touched the little gold bells to make them ring.

'For you, my love,' he whispered softly, then he shut his eyes tight and wiped them clear.

When his mind was finally set, the candle maker lifted down the coat from its hook and swiftly threw it around his shoulders. Then he pulled the hood firmly over his head and went to the stable, where he lit the lantern and stepped out with the horse and cart into the cold winter's night.

The candle maker led the horse in a blaze of light through the falling snow and down the muddy lane to the edge of the village. When he saw the first few cottages, he paused for a while, too afraid to continue any further. He wanted to turn around and go back to his home where he felt safe, but he had worked all year for this night and remembered the words of the ringmaster. For his plan to work he could not pass through the village in secret. He knew that he had to be seen. He had to draw all the villagers out from their homes towards him and, perhaps he hoped, each other as well.

From the seat of the cart he lifted down the black bag that the ringmaster had given him, and from it he took a shiny brass hand bell with a polished oak handle. He rubbed the sleeve of the coat over its surface and saw his face reflected in the bell. He forced himself to smile, feeling that people would welcome a cheerful face more than his usual frown, but he dropped the idea and sighed glumly, as he knew that they would see through such a false expression. Eventually, however, he managed to shake any foolish doubts that he held from his mind and nodded purposefully to himself.

50

As the snow eased, the candle maker walked on beside the horse and cart. When they entered the village, he began swinging the bell, quietly at first but then louder until it rang out across the whole district.

Faces soon appeared at the windows. Slowly, the cottage doors opened and the villagers came out to see the colourful bearded man, who had suddenly appeared among them and was now standing in a pool of brightness and sounding a bell that broke the silence of the night. They gathered around the cart, curious to know the stranger and his purpose. Some patted the horse and stroked its mane. Others looked over the cart and its painted decorations of sparkling silver stars and golden sunbeams.

The candle maker greeted everyone who approached him and wished them well for the coming year. He listened to all their troubles, which the present time of shortage and hardship had brought them, then he moved to the rear of the cart, where he passed out bundles of candles to every villager. He sat the children on his knee and let them tug at his beard to see if it was real. They told him their names and what they hoped for in the future. The children instinctively searched in the pockets of the coat but they were empty. The candle maker tried to reassure them that winter would soon pass and they would again play in the sun, but he regretted that he had not brought some special treat for each child.

More villagers came out towards the candle maker. One cautiously took the offering and hid it in his coat, then hurried back to his home like a frightened rabbit. Another stood from a distance with folded arms and shrugged his shoulders, while others turned their backs on the candle maker but not before taking their share from the cart. The boy who had helped in the workshop appeared in the crowd with his parents and sister. They thanked the candle maker for his gift, then the boy's father whispered to his son. Eagerly the boy ran back to their cottage and quickly returned with a jug of wine to toast each other's health and a bunch of carrots to feed the horse.

Beside the road a group of girls watched the candle maker, while they nervously giggled to each other. There were no flowers to be found so they picked mistletoe from a nearby elm tree and placed it in their hair. Then they bashfully approached the candle maker, believing that a kiss on the stranger's cheek, and a posy for himself, would bring them luck.

Next, a young mother came forward and proudly showed the baby in her arms to the candle maker. When the child's eyes eventually found the stranger's great bearded face, it instantly screamed with fright and burst into tears, while the woman shielded and removed her offspring from his view in disgust.

Lastly, an elderly couple struggled towards the cart through the snow. They took the last of the stranger's candles and blessed him repeatedly for his kindness. The candle maker watched the couple return to their cottage, as though the years had suddenly fallen away from their tired aged bodies, and a new dawn broke ahead of them to mark the beginning of another day together.

Six

When he returned home, the candle maker stabled the horse, staggered through to the cottage and fell facedown, exhausted onto his bed. The strain of being around people had again got to him and he slept restlessly, dreaming of all those in the world that he had not helped, and others who had spent the night in darkness.

When he woke, however, a new idea came to the candle maker. He remembered how the children's faces had brightened when they had first seen him, but all that he could offer them were a few words of comfort. He wanted to give the children something that would make his visit special to each of them. The light of a candle may hold a child's interest for a short while, but its flame cannot be touched and never lasts forever. Next time, he thought, he would leave behind a little of himself – just for the children.

The candle maker was familiar with the district where he lived, but other regions further than his own experience were a mystery to him. He thought that the entire country must be vast, and the world beyond was perhaps a thousand times that size. In one night he had only visited his own village, and he realised that it would take some small miracle to venture even a little further. Yet he did feel that with practice he could visit a second village in the same time the following year, and perhaps even another after that, for the candle maker had yet to discover how far he could travel in a single night.

Another problem that he saw was the amount of work that it would take to make enough candles for every home in the district. Even with the boy's help there had only been enough for those in his own village, but he knew that with a little improvement to their methods they could make many more in the coming year.

The candle maker decided not to dwell any further on these difficulties, believing that they served no purpose in his mission and only obstructed his progress. The most important task, he thought, was to make a space in the cottage where he could work in secret on his new plan.

He cleared half the main room and divided it with a curtain so that even the boy would not know his scheme. Then he set up a table and chair before the window and brought in a few tools from the workshop. From then on, every morning when the boy had gone home after work, the candle maker would spend a few hours watching the birds and animals in the garden outside, and he captured their likenesses in wooden carvings before retiring to bed.

That season the candle maker and the boy did produce more candles than they had the previous year. Many more, in fact, and yet they did not work an hour longer each night, but remained steady and constant in their tasks from dusk until dawn. Together they got to know each other's ways and decided what jobs suited them best. As he became more skilled, the boy would suggest ideas of his own that at first the candle maker thought were foolish and would not work, but the candle maker was often proved wrong and quite surprised when they succeeded.

One evening the boy crushed bunches of lavender into oil and mixed it with the wax. When these candles were lit, they filled the cottage with a summer perfume.

'What's that smell?' asked the candle maker, as he entered the workshop and saw the boy sniffing the fragrance of a lighted candle on the bench. The boy looked up nervously.

'For a lady's dressing table, sir.'

The candle maker thought for a moment, then he grudgingly nodded his approval and returned to his seat in the cottage.

When autumn approached, the candle maker would leave the boy to work alone all night in the workshop, while he sat at his table, such was his belief in the boy's ability as a chandler. At the same time, however, the candle maker felt that perhaps he was no longer needed in the workshop. Sometimes he thought that he might be holding the boy back in his work, and possibly even obstructing the progress that he was making in his trade. Yet the boy would occasionally call out for some help, which pleased the candle maker and proved to him that he was still useful.

As the year drew to a close, the candle maker spent more and more hours at his table behind the curtain. Meanwhile, the boy made the workshop his own. He also toured the district with the handcart, gathering wax for the following year. When their work was finished, they thanked each other for all that they had achieved together, and it pleased them both to know that there would be candles for the whole village that winter – and many more besides.

'I shall visit soon,' said the candle maker, as they parted company. 'I promise.'

'I'll look forward to seeing you,' replied the boy, and he left the cottage for the last time that year.

As soon as the boy was gone, the candle maker pulled a great sack from behind the curtain and set it beside his chair by the fire. He spent the next few days carefully painting each likeness, while he smiled and chuckled to himself, and smoked his clay pipe and drank his mulled wine. Every image that he completed seemed to have its own peculiar character, and he would quietly chatter to every one in turn and mimic their behaviour, before carefully replacing each in the sack.

Alone in his own house and working peacefully by the fire, he felt that he was himself again. He could say what he liked and act as he pleased without fearing the judgment of others. Yet he knew that his behaviour was not right for the common world. Still, he hoped that his true manners would be welcomed by the villagers, as a cheerful distraction from the strains of their everyday life, and they might please the children in such a cold and dark season of the year.

On the evening of the chosen night, the candle maker once more lifted down the long red winter coat from its hook behind the door and slung it around his shoulders. Again he stepped out in his black leather riding boots, and again he rang the bell throughout the village. This time, however, there was no hesitating by the villagers. They poured out from their homes through the snow to meet him, the young and old alike, wrapped up in their winter clothes. As he drove the cart through the village, they eagerly followed him, greeting each other as they went, and they offered their neighbours good wishes and happiness for the coming year.

At the far end of the village, the candle maker pulled the cart to a halt and passed out candles to every villager. Then he lifted the great sack down from the rear of the cart and beckoned the children forward. They approached him nervously with serious expressions, but their faces soon cheered as the candle maker reached into the sack and handed a gift to every child. Delightedly they ran back to the arms of their parents and showed them what they had been given. Then they all turned to thank the candle maker, but he was already back at the reins of the cart and driving out of the village into the night.

The cart trundled along the road under overhanging trees that leaned lower than usual, as they were heavy with snow. The candle maker's lantern lit up the branches from below, and the road beneath him and a little ahead, but further on and behind was hidden in complete darkness. He drove onward unsure of how far he was travelling or how long the journey was taking. He knew that he would come upon another village or dwelling sooner or later, but the trees were closing in thicker around him, and the road narrowed into nothing more than a muddy lane, which had not seen a horse and rider or cart for many years. The candle maker decided that he was surely lost and must turn back to the village, but when he pulled at the reins the horse continued trotting purposefully forward. The candle maker called out to the horse and pulled harder on the reins, but the horse did not stop and again only quickened its step through the trees.

'Whoa! Whoa!' cried the candle maker, as branches

swiped at him and dropped heavy lumps of snow onto his head and shoulders. The cartwheels bumped over the uneven ground. The candle maker struggled with the horse, but he could hold the reins no longer and eventually let them slip through his fingers. One last jolt threw him off his seat and a great downpour of snow buried him in the back of the cart.

After a moment the candle maker appeared dazed and shivering from beneath a mound of frozen white flakes. He shook the snow from his hair and beard, and brushed his coat.

'What are you trying to do to me?' he shouted at the horse, then he stood up and realised that the cart had stopped. The thick trees were gone and the road ahead was clear, and the candle maker climbed back onto his seat, grumbling aloud.

'If we carry on like this, we'll never get – ' Suddenly he broke off as he noticed two shrouded figures, who were standing huddled in the doorway of a tiny crooked cottage by the side of the road. The couple approached in silence, while the candle maker assumed that they must think him a very odd fellow indeed, as they had obviously heard him talking to the horse. Nervously, he watched them draw nearer. They touched the horse with their bony fingers and circled the cart, examining its every detail. Their curious attention began to make the candle maker feel quite uneasy. Cautiously, he picked up the reins and was about to drive the cart away when one of them removed the shawl that covered their face and spoke to him.

'I've heard of you,' said an old man, smiling up towards the candle maker. 'Some said you would not come, but I knew you would.' Then he turned to the old woman who was standing beside him.

'You see?' he continued. 'I told you he would visit us.'

'Bless you, sir,' cried the woman with her hands clasped together. 'Bless you!'

The candle maker was relieved that the couple were not about to cause him any harm. He quickly grabbed a bundle of candles and handed them to the woman. Her face suddenly lit up as though the candles she was holding were already alight. There were deep lines cut in her forehead and her cheeks fell in over the few teeth that she still had in her mouth. The man was just as thin and frail. His eyes were surrounded by wide dark rings and above them his brows drooped sadly on either side of his face. They were the poorest people that the candle maker had ever seen, and their hard lives had aged them more than their years. Yet they were not without hope. No matter how harsh life had become for them they remained true to each other, and by each other's side they now stood before the candle maker. Perhaps his visit and the gift of candles had reminded them of more joyful times, which they had shared in light, warmth and happiness. Perhaps also they would look to the future, no matter how uncertain it was, without fear and in good spirits for whatever it brought them. The couple thanked the candle maker a dozen times and returned to their home with their arms around each other, and the woman's head resting on the man's shoulder. As the door closed, light poured out through the windows, and the old cottage that had looked so uninviting to the outsider now took on an altogether more welcoming appearance.

The candle maker smiled to himself. He thought deeply for a moment, but when he saw the horse staring blankly back at him, his eyes and lips narrowed and he glared at the animal with cautious annoyance.

'Well?' he called impatiently. 'What are you waiting for?' Immediately the horse set off down the road with the candle maker again struggling to hold the reins.

A little further on there were more cottages, one or two at first, but then a row that led down to the crossroads of another village. When the candle maker rang the bell, again people came out to meet him, and again he passed out candles for every home and presents to the children. Some greeted him as if he were one of their own family, while others were more wary about the stranger. However, most soon warmed towards his cheerful greeting when they saw that he wanted nothing from them and meant them no harm. They too eventually smiled in his favour and waved him onward, as though they were encouraging him to go still further on his journey.

A light shower of snow began to fall as the candle maker drove through the next village. It was larger than his own, and there were many shops and businesses of all kinds along the main street. He passed a gang of navvies who were returning from work, tired but not so beaten by their day's labour digging canals that they could not happily raise their caps to the candle maker. Shopkeepers locking up for the night also found a moment to greet him as he went by. Two large farm hands crashed bruised and bloodied through the door of the village tavern, and out into the mud and slush. They staggered drunkenly to their feet, and were about to continue their fistfight, but could only laugh at each other and their foolish quarrel when they saw the candle maker in the light of the lantern.

The candle maker drove onward, passed homes and through villages that he had never visited before. Still people waved and even cheered to him as he went by. They greeted him merrily without knowing who he was or why he was there, and for no reason other than it pleased them to do so. Then they thanked him warmly for his gift and took the memory of him back inside their homes.

***

By midnight the candle maker found himself heading towards the centre of a small market town. The lantern was dimming to a faint glow, and the few people that he passed did not notice him steering the cart silently through the snowy unlit streets. The horse needed rest, and the candle maker was also tiring, so he pulled the cart to a halt on the opposite side of the street from a large inn, just as the flame in the lantern went out.

The only light came from the windows of the inn, where inside there was music playing, and people were singing and laughing. The light shone out onto the courtyard of the inn and across the street, but the candle maker remained in the shadows, sitting on the cart and listening to the music and the voices that filled the air outside. His spirits fell a little as he thought that he was now of an age and character that could not take part in such gatherings, yet he imagined how much the guests inside were enjoying the evening and each other's company. He sang quietly to the music, but it was a tune that he had never heard before and soon gave up, thinking it foolish to try and follow a song that was unknown to him. Neither, he thought, would he be able to join in the dance, as whatever steps that he had trodden before he had long forgotten, and even they would probably have been replaced by those of a new jig.

As he sat glumly in the dark, the candle maker noticed a dark shape shuffling towards the door of the inn. He could not tell if it was a man or a woman, a child or an animal, but the shape was certainly alive and settled down on the steps beside the door, then placed a bowl out in front of itself.

There was a faint rumbling sound in the distance. The candle maker turned and looked up the street as a coach drawn by two grey horses made its way through the snow towards him. The coach stopped outside the inn. Immediately a footman leapt from its rear, set the step and opened the door for the passenger inside. He bowed humbly as a young man in the finest evening clothes climbed out and hurriedly made his way up the steps of the inn. The young man stopped in alarm when he saw the dark shape leaning forward towards him. Cautiously, he lifted his cane and with its point he pushed the shape firmly away from him, back against the wall of the inn, then he quickly went inside. The footman returned to his place, the driver cracked his whip and the coach set off again, disappearing around the side of the building.

The candle maker watched as the dark shape lowered to resume its position against the wall. No flame would warm the heart of this hopeless creature, he decided, but there was nothing left in the cart to give, and, even if there were, the candle maker was uncertain that it would be of any comfort to the poor homeless soul.

By now the candle maker had travelled several miles from his cottage. He felt that he could journey many more in the night hours that remained, but he believed that there was no sense in pulling an empty cart from door to door with nothing to leave behind. No one would understand him, he thought, or why he was there and what he was doing, so instead he stood up and turned his back on the inn to relight the lantern and return home.

It took him a few minutes to adjust the wick and set the wax, but eventually he struck a spark from his flint box and light spilled out from the lantern, across the street and brightened up every corner of the town square. Suddenly he heard voices behind him and what sounded like a waterfall. He spun around to face the inn and saw a crowd of people standing at the door, and others in the courtyard who were leaving the dance. They gazed in amazement at the light. Some called out in astonishment, while the rest put their hands together and applauded the spectacle.

The candle maker was just as surprised by the reception that he was given as he was by the people who were offering him their appreciation. He had never seen people like these before. The ladies wore long dresses of the finest silk, some trimmed with lace, that widened from their waists to the ground. Their hair was dressed neatly and tied with ribbons and jewels, while pearls shone out from their ears and around their powdered necks. Most of the gentlemen stood in their smart black and white evening clothes, although some were more colourful in red tunics with gold braid and buttons. They were young army officers, who were enjoying their last evening of leave with their sweethearts before departing for duty in some far off land. It pleased them all to see the candle maker standing on the cart beneath the blazing lantern. They waved at him and he returned the gesture, although unsure of their reason for doing so and the effect that his presence in the town square was having on the gathering before him. Somehow, the candle maker and the light that surrounded him drew the people closer together. Couples held hands or embraced then gazed into each other's eyes smiling. The rest exchanged their compliments of the season, and all agreed that there was no finer way to end the evening than with them all assembled outside the snow-covered inn, which was now bathed in light.

As if from nowhere, a jolly middle-aged man with a great moustache appeared beside the cart. He wore the same red jacket as the young officers, but his was tighter around his large stomach and heavy with medals on his chest. He had hurried across the street unnoticed by the candle maker and was now holding out his hand for him to shake with his face beaming with pleasure.

'Bravo!' said the old Colonel, glancing up at the lantern. 'I say, bravo, sir. Splendid. Splendid!'

The candle maker bent down and shook the Colonel's hand. He smiled back at him in thanks, then he realised that his visit was not only welcomed by the young and old, but also rich and poor alike. These people in their fine clothes, he thought, had all eaten and drunk well that evening, and still they took pleasure in seeing him on a winter's night. Now, he realised, he could bring some happiness to anyone who gave a little of themselves to him, be it a kindly smile or a simple wave, and each, he believed, might turn that affection towards their loved ones, neighbours or even a complete stranger. Perhaps then, he felt, they would reflect on their past twelve months and consider not simply those less fortunate, but all their fellow beings, every one, even if it was just for a moment, and only on one night of the year.

Suddenly the Colonel turned from the candle maker and looked up the street. The candle maker raised himself up under the lantern, and he heard in the distance the sound of many drums approaching. Again the Colonel nodded with approval to the candle maker but quickly dashed back to the steps of the inn, where everyone listened with excitement as thunderous drums boomed out so loud that they shook the ground and knocked snow off the rooftops. The drums were soon joined by the sound of many flutes and bugles, and out of the darkness rode a Captain on a black stallion followed by a hundred men in uniform. The Captain's eyes were dark and lifeless, and he bore a great scar across his cheek from his ear to his chin. The men who marched behind him were no more than nervous boys.

As they passed the inn, the music was deafening. The Captain pulled his horse aside and allowed his men to march before him. Some wore swords from their belts, while others carried muskets over their shoulders. The crowd on the inn steps cheered with pride, or waved with tears in their eyes, as the battalion entered the full glare of the lantern. The candle maker saw every one of their young faces, and he waved to them all and smiled.

The soldiers did not smile. Some dared only to look at the candle maker from the corner of their eye, fearing that the Captain would discipline them severely for breaking the ranks. However, within the light that now surrounded them, they took on a calmer appearance, and their expressions no longer showed any sign of fear.

The Captain stared blankly at the candle maker from his horse across the street. He saw his red coat with its gold buttons and wondered for a moment if he could be a member of his own regiment. The Captain instinctively knew that this bearded figure was not a soldier, and yet his presence and greeting seemed to have a positive effect on his men that few commanding officers could match. He had cheered them and, if only for a short while, made each forget the battle that they were marching towards, and from which many would certainly not return.

As the music faded and the last man left the town square, the candle maker turned to the Captain, who was still glaring at him menacingly and motionless from his horse across the street. The crowd on the inn steps were saying goodnight to one another and leaving in coaches, which had arrived to take them to their homes. The candle maker stood nervously, thinking that the Captain might be angry at him for distracting his men. Yet the Captain almost managed to smile himself as he sat upright in his saddle, raised his right hand to his forehead and saluted the candle maker for what he had done.

The candle maker smiled. He nodded and waved back before the Captain quickly turned his horse and rode off into the night.

The last to leave the inn was the young gentleman with the cane, who the candle maker had first seen when he had arrived in the town square. Again he stood beside the dark shape against the wall, where it had remained unnoticed by anyone throughout the procession. He saw the candle maker, who raised his hand towards him, but the gentleman turned away as the young woman who he was waiting for appeared at the door.

The woman stepped out into the light and waved cheerfully to the candle maker, then she noticed the dark shape against the wall. The woman whispered a few words into the gentleman's ear, and, before they walked off together towards their carriage, the young man took out his purse and dropped a few coins in the beggar's bowl.

Seven

By the time the sun rose again the candle maker was back at home and sitting by his fire, puffing on his clay pipe and supping his mulled wine. He was tired from his night's work but it was a good feeling of tiredness, a feeling that he had achieved as much as he had wanted in one night and more besides. He looked around the cottage and felt that he had been away from his home for many days, perhaps even weeks, and yet he knew that in all that time he had not seen the sun climb above the horizon. He did not know how far he had travelled but firmly believed that even with the old carthorse more miles were possible, and that he could visit many other villages and towns that lay still further away. A broad smile appeared across the candle maker's face when he thought of all the people that he had met on his round, and he chuckled to himself when he remembered how surprised they had been to see him. However, his face fell a little when realised that he could not stay long in their company if he was to cover more ground. Perhaps, he thought, they might not warm to him as much if they only got a brief glance of him passing. What if they did not even see him and only found the things that he had left behind when they woke in the morning? The candle maker drew on his great white beard and wondered if people would give any thought at all as to who had left candles at their door and presents for their children on one night in the middle of winter. Furthermore, what would it mean to him if people believed that the gifts had come from some loving relative or a kindly neighbour? Yet would that matter so much, he thought?

As the morning sun streamed in through the window, the candle maker stretched out his arms and gave a large loud yawn, then he sank back in his chair and fell into a deep sleep.

He rested over the next few days, tending to the horse and stable and tidying the workshop, and when the last snow of winter had melted the boy returned to help him. While they prepared for the season's work, the candle maker would leave the cottage in the afternoons and drive the horse and cart across the district in search of all the supplies and materials that he could find. The boy had collected a good supply of wax the previous year, but the candle maker found more from hives further away. In addition, the old melting pots were in need of repair, some tools required sharpening and there were no flax bales for the wicks.

He found most of what he needed from the tinkers and knife grinders who regularly travelled along the roads between the villages. However, the vast fields of flax that had once provided the whole district with enough linen for a year were now ploughed ready for planting vegetables, or given over to keeping pigs or grazing by cattle and sheep. The candle maker asked one young farmhand where he could find a few bales of the plant that he needed for his wicks, but the lad just shook his head as though he had never seen or even heard of the crop in his life. What had happened to the countryside that he knew as a boy, thought the candle maker? The landscape appeared the same but was surely changing. The spring colours did not appear in the fields and the land was dark, as though grey clouds had formed in the sky above and hidden the sun from view.

As the weeks past, the candle maker grew more and more anxious that he and the boy might not be able to make any candles that year. Moreover, without wicks on which to dry the melted wax they could not progress any further in their work. He spent the evenings brooding by the fire, but still tried to keep busy by sewing together scraps of cloth and forming them into rag dolls. However, each pass of the needle seemed to be more of a strain on his eyes than the last. He could only work for a few minutes at a time before dropping the work on his lap and sinking back into his chair with his eyes closed tight and his head aching. He could see the room about him and even the faintest stars far off through the window, but anything that he brought close up to his eyes was just a blur. He found that if he held the work at arm's length he could see it clearly, but then it was too far away to be precise. Often he sighed in hopelessness at how little he produced each night and was sometimes unfairly abrupt to the boy, who could do no more than tidy the benches in the workshop and sweep the floor. Eventually, however, the candle maker decided that he would search the entire district, and further if necessary, for whatever flax he could find. He prepared the cart and packed a week's provisions, then told the boy that he would call for him when he returned.

The candle maker drove the cart several miles across the district and managed to find a few stems of flax growing wild by the roadside. He found some more at the edge of fields and beside the hedgerows, those that had been sown in a previous season and now remained to grow freely among the nettles. The candle maker collected every stem that he could find, yet he secretly knew that there was not enough for a year's work and these few remaining plants were of such poor quality that they would only hold the dullest flame.

As another day of searching ended without success, the candle maker drove the cart down into a valley, where there were a few scattered hamlets. He slowly approached the houses in the distance and passed an old barn in a field nearby. He pulled the cart to a halt and saw that part of the barn's roof had collapsed. Its doors were hanging loose from their hinges and swinging freely in the early evening breeze. The field had been abandoned and was now overgrown, and the barn had been left unattended, but the candle maker decided to look inside for anything that he might find useful. He trod carefully on the uneven ground, and through weeds and long blades of grass that came up to his middle. The barn's doors creaked and banged together in the wind. As the clouds above him grew darker, the candle maker suddenly felt that he was not alone and being watched by someone hiding in the field. Nervously, he turned back to the road and saw the horse standing calmly, still harnessed to the cart. The candle maker thought that perhaps he should not go any further, but then a familiar smell passed across his face from inside the barn. He breathed in the aroma deeply through his nose and decided that he must continue, and so squeezed through the space between the doors.

The candle maker stood motionless in the barn, while his eyes adjusted to the darkness. He saw the beams from the roof and its thatch, which had fallen through to the floor. He walked in further and climbed over the ruins, then stumbled on the fragile structure, which brought down more thatch and sent a cloud of dust and cobwebs on top of him. The candle maker coughed and sneezed, and cursed on his knees. He got to his feet and brushed himself off, while the dust cleared to reveal, stacked neatly against the far wall, bales of flax under what roof that remained to keep them dry. They had been grown and tied by someone, but that someone's tools had been left rusting on the floor, so it was clear they were bales that no one wanted. The candle maker examined the stems. It was good flax, straight and long, and yet, he thought, why was it of no use to anyone but him? The candle maker shivered and suddenly became scared as he realised that the world was changing into something that he did not understand.

Outside on the road the horse was disturbed. Cold wind blew in through the barn, while an owl hooted high up in the broken rafters.

Quickly the candle maker picked up as many bales as he could carry and ran from the barn like a thief. He threw the bales into the cart, grabbed the reins and turned the horse back up the road on which they had travelled. He tried desperately to quicken the horse, wishing to get away from the scene as swiftly as possible, but the horse would not walk any faster. As he drove on, the candle maker felt that he had committed some dreadful crime, but then, he thought, what crime was there in taking a few bales of flax that had been left to rot in a derelict barn? The further the cart climbed up the hill, the more sure he became that he had caused no harm to anyone. Furthermore, he cheered himself as he thought of the many candles that he could now make and all the people who would have light next winter. As the cart reached the top of the hill, the candle maker felt much easier with himself and dismissed any thoughts of wrongdoing from his mind. He looked back to the barn, which had conveniently disappeared in the fading light, but when he turned around the horse suddenly reared to a halt before a group of men, who blocked the road and were holding burning torches and farm tools like weapons.

They were hard men who lived and worked hard lives on the land. Their beards were long, their skin was burnt almost black by the sun, and they had no pity in their eyes for strangers or thieves – or both.

The candle maker froze. The men watched him sternly but in silence. He tried to mutter some apology for stealing their crops and begged them not to harm him. However, even if he could have managed more than a few words, the men ignored his excuses and set about recovering their property. They had a determined look in their eyes and would think nothing of beating unconscious, or worse, the villain who had crossed them. They crowded nearer and examined the horse. They crawled over every inch of the cart and carefully picked through the candle maker's pockets, his supplies and the bales of flax that he had stolen. Finally, they got down from the cart and whispered to each other, while nodding menacingly in the candle maker's direction.

The candle maker trembled with fear. He began

breathing heavily, as though each breath he took would be his last. He retched in terror, sweating and was violently sick over the side of the cart. The men watched him closely but showed no sign of pity.

The candle maker lifted his head and sat slumped in the cart, shamefully wiping his mouth. The men sighed regrettably to each other, then they calmly moved to the side of the road, allowing the candle maker to continue on his journey. Clearly he was not the villain that they were looking for, and neither, they were forced to admit, had he anything that belonged to them.

The candle maker picked up the reins with his hands still shaking and drove the cart over the brow of the hill, and out of sight of the valley and the men who had stopped him. He travelled for several miles in the dark, not wishing any light to attract attention to himself. The countryside was deserted. The moon lit the road before him, and there was no sound except the horse's hooves, the wheels of the cart on the road and a few faint muffled calls from below where he was sitting. The candle maker did not hear the cries at first, as he was thinking deeply about the events of the evening. However, soon a louder and more frantic knocking sound joined the calls.

The candle maker pulled the cart to a halt and listened carefully. He looked around him but found no one in sight, and he could not imagine where they might be hiding.

'Who's there?' he called.

'Let me out. Let me out!' cried a feeble voice from under him, and the candle maker suddenly leapt to his feet in surprise. He lifted the wooden seat of the cart and the small head and arms of a little man popped out, who was gasping for breath.

'Oh, I thought I was a goner there,' said the little man, wheezing and coughing.

'Who are you?' asked the candle maker sternly. 'What are you doing in there?'

The little man climbed out of the space beneath the seat and pulled out his bag of belongings, which was almost as big as him.

'Hiding for my life,' he said, closing the seat and sitting down exhausted. 'That was nearly my own coffin.'

The candle maker sat beside him, lit a small lantern and studied the little man closely. He was fully grown but no bigger than the boy who helped in the workshop. He twitched nervously and seemed to view everything around him with suspicion.

'You're the one they were looking for,' said the candle maker earnestly, but the little man remained silent. 'Those men, it's you they're after!'

'They'd have killed me for sure,' replied the little man. 'And for no reason.'

'You stole from them.'

'I did not!' snapped the little man, so firmly that the candle maker was rocked back in his seat.

They both sat for a moment in silence. The little man sighed to himself, while the candle maker waited to hear his explanation. Eventually, the little man spoke, uttering his words despairingly.

'When something goes missing, they always blame the likes of me. It seems every misfortune they suffer is my doing. I stole nothing from those men, yet they accused me of committing an offence. And there is no arguing against their word.'

The little man swung round to the candle maker and

looked him in the eye.

'Believe me, I am innocent of the charge they laid upon me, but, believe me also, I am guilty of another.'

'What wrong have you done?' asked the candle maker, who was now shocked by what he was hearing.

'Difference is my felony,' said the little man bluntly. 'I am not the same as others and so they look upon me as suspect. My shape offends them, as do my actions over which I have no control. When they are wronged, they turn on me and drive me away. I have lost my home and business, and through no fault of my own except the form in which I am forced to exist – and the shadow I cast on this world.'

As they talked further, the candle maker could see that the little man had been unjustly treated, but he also saw something of himself in his new companion. They both knew what it was like to be shunned by society, and when they had felt secure among people it had been a short-lived affair that ended badly. They saw no hope in remaining part of any community, yet neither had given up on themselves and still held a deep desire to belong in human company.

'What was your business?' asked the candle maker, as he came to realise that he had found an unlikely soul mate.

'Cloth is my business,' replied the little man. 'I can weave it, cut it, sew it. I'm a tailor. Or at least I was, but, as if times were not bad enough in my trade, and given my present hardship, I am not sure that I will be again.'

The candle maker and the tailor sat together on the cart under the stars and talked the night through. Gradually, an idea formed in the candle maker's head. Just before the sun appeared above the horizon, he found the courage to offer the tailor his proposition.

'Do not pity me,' said the tailor harshly. 'I'll take nothing I have not earned.'

'I can give you a home and work,' returned the candle maker, but the tailor was still reluctant to accept. He had been wronged enough times in the past to trust a stranger, and yet he also found his new acquaintance agreeable.

The candle maker sighed. He thought deeply and uneasily. After a short while, he was eventually forced to confide in the tailor something that until that moment he had not even admitted to himself.

'I need help,' he said finally. 'I'm not able to complete my undertakings alone. I'm asking if you will help me.'

The day was breaking, but the sun had not yet appeared in the sky.

The tailor thought about his life. He had no family or friends, and no idea of where to settle next. He knew how difficult it was to live and work alone, and could see no better, or indeed any other, opportunity before him. Moreover, he was tired. The years that he had spent making a life for himself, only to have it destroyed in an instant, had taken their toll on his mind and body, and now all that he wished for was a small quiet space where he could work and think clearly again. He too was in need of help, and so, without any further persuading by the candle maker, the tailor accepted his offer.

The two men nodded to each other in agreement, with a shared understanding of the task that lay ahead. As the sun rose, they set off down the road again, and a new day began that they had both thought they would never see.

Eight

When the candle maker and the tailor returned to the cottage, they found that the front door was slightly open. The candle maker pulled the cart to a halt and cautiously approached his home, fearing that he was the one who was now being robbed. He signalled to the tailor to go around to the back of the cottage and catch anyone leaving. Slowly, the candle maker pushed open the door and crept inside. He could hear movement in the workshop. Someone was in there. Immediately he seized a poker from beside the fire and prepared to take on the villain. He inched further forward and raised the poker above his head, growing more and more angry that anyone should enter his house uninvited and take his belongings. Finally, calling out in rage, he swung open the workshop door and found the boy dipping candles into a pot of melted wax. The boy cried out in fear and almost knocked over the pot, while the candle maker sighed, put a hand on his chest and felt as though he was about to faint.

'What are you doing here?' asked the candle maker, annoyed but equally relieved that there was no thief to confront.

'I wanted to start work again,' said the boy.

'We can't work,' returned the candle maker angrily.

'There are no wicks.'

He put down the poker then saw what the boy was using to draw out the melted wax. There were more lengths of the same, cut to size and carefully laid out on the bench. The candle maker picked one up and rubbed it through his fingers, examining the strands.

'It spins well,' said the candle maker, as he gazed on the new substance. 'What is it?'

'A merchant passed through the village two days ago,' replied the boy. 'I thought we could use it.'

'Does it light?' asked the candle maker. The boy nodded and turned to a few candles that were already burning at different lengths on a shelf at the far end of the workshop. Their flames were perfect, large and unflickering, and the candle maker could see that these wicks were as good, if not better, than any made of flax.

'Is this all we have?' asked the candle maker, pointing to the few wicks on the bench. The boy rose from his seat and stood aside. On the floor behind him were two large square sacks of the same white material. It spilled out, loose and in little round balls, from the corner of one sack. The candle maker reached for a handful to study closely. Each ball was about the size of a pigeon's egg, like wool but finer and softer than feather down. The sacks were tied tightly with rope, and there were no markings on them to say from where they had come. Only one large word painted on each sack told the name of this new and mysterious fibre, 'Cotton'.

The candle maker thought for a moment. The tailor entered the workshop through the rear door with his bag on his shoulder. The candle maker was unhappy about using the new material, not knowing its origin, but he had to admit that, given the shortage of flax in the district, there was no alternative. He turned to the tailor, who was now staring at the sacks with his eyes wide open.

'What's your opinion, master tailor?' asked the candle maker. 'Has the boy bought good?'

The tailor nodded approvingly.

'Very well then,' said the candle maker, and he dusted his hands off with a clap and eagerly rubbed them together. 'Let's get started, shall we?'

The candle maker left the boy to experiment with the new wicks and showed the tailor through to the cottage, where the little man inquisitively inspected his new home. Eventually, he assured himself that it was a secure and safe place in which to live, and the candle maker helped him clear a space by the wall beside the fire, where the tailor stowed his belongings and made his bed. The candle maker lit the fire and sat in his chair on the opposite side, while the tailor perched on a short three-legged stool and examined the poorly stitched rag dolls that lay on the floor beside him.

'*You* made these?' asked the tailor.

'My eyes are not what they were,' replied the candle maker glumly. He held the list that he was making in front of him and stared blankly at the paper.

The tailor sighed and shook his head. He swung his bag in front of him and searched inside, where he found a collection of twisted wires and glass. He pulled one of the wires free of the others and handed it to the candle maker, who had never seen a pair of spectacles before. The tailor motioned to the candle maker to lift them up to his face and secure them around his ears. Cautiously, the candle maker gazed through the crescent shaped lenses and suddenly the list that he was writing appeared before him clear and sharp.

'Oh!' he exclaimed in complete surprise, and he raised the glasses and replaced them on his nose several times to see the difference that they made to his sight.

'Splendid!' he said to himself. Then, without a word of thanks to the tailor, he continued writing his list with all the eagerness for his task that he seemed to have lost over the recent weeks.

The tailor shook his head, and began unpicking stitches and repairing the worst of the rag dolls. Later, he made a small hand loom for himself in which he would sit for hours at a time, throwing the shuttle from side to side through the warp threads and weaving cloth a yard wide. At work he was a different person. He kept his eyes fixed firmly on the loom, and there was no hesitation in his movements or tremors on his hands. He cut the cloth to size and sewed and stuffed more dolls and other soft playthings, while the candle maker sat at his table by the window, shaping and painting his creatures from wood. The tailor also made little bags, which the candle maker would fill with toys and leave at the homes of children who were sleeping when he called.

Meanwhile, the boy ran the workshop. He made more candles than ever that year, but he chose to work during the day and return home in the evenings. The candle maker and the tailor, however, laboured on late into the night and did not stop until dawn. They paused only to eat and sleep. When the boy arrived early in the morning, the candle maker would spend an hour or two helping in the workshop before he rested, but as the year past he could see that his help was no longer needed. The boy had mastered his trade, and the candle maker felt the same pride and regret that his father had sensed when he had passed his work over to a younger man.

After their meal the candle maker and the tailor would sit by the fire and talk. Often they shared a glass of mulled wine and told each other the stories of their lives. They found that their similarities were as many as their differences. They were likeminded in some of their views but opposite in others, and they would argue and agree passionately in equal measures. Gradually, the tailor came to feel quite comfortable in his new home. He wanted for nothing but was still suspicious of the candle maker's reasons for what he had chosen to do for the rest of his life.

'Why do you give so much of yourself each year?' asked the tailor one evening.

'Because it pleases me,' replied the candle maker firmly.

The tailor remained unconvinced, and just shrugged and turned to the fire.

'You don't like people very much, do you?' returned the candle maker, glancing over the rim of his spectacles.

'I don't like people because they don't like me,' replied the tailor. He stared thoughtfully into the fire, and the candle maker went back to his list.

'Perhaps it's the other way round.'

The tailor did not reply but turned his head to hear more.

The candle maker leant forward in his chair and looked passionately in the tailor's face.

'Come with me tomorrow night,' he said eagerly. 'Perhaps I can restore your belief in mankind.'

The tailor thought for a moment. He was reluctant to accept, but at the same time he was secretly curious about the candle maker's journey.

'I may be recognised.' said the tailor. 'Those men will still be looking for me.'

'Then we shall disguise you,' replied the candle maker.

'My size will betray me.'

'Some people only see the surface of a person and look no further. You must appear before them in a manner they would least expect.'

'What sort of manner?' asked the tailor.

'Cheerful, perhaps?' suggested the candle maker, and he sat back in his chair with a broad smile on his face.

The tailor grumbled to himself and turned back to the fire. He was still doubtful of what the candle maker had told him about the earlier rounds, and yet, as he gazed into the flames, something deep down inside him longed to see the effect that the candle maker had on people and what it was that he brought into their lives.

The next day the first snow of winter began falling, which continued until late afternoon. The tailor watched the snow through the cottage window, while the candle maker and the boy carried great sacks of candles and toys out from the workshop, and loaded them onto the cart. The tailor wondered how each snowflake could form into the same six-pointed star, and yet, as they stuck to the glass in front of him, he could see that their exact shapes were all different. From a distance they appeared identical but when closely examined he found that no two were the same. He looked out further across the snow-covered fields and realised that every frozen crystal was unique, and that those now melting into drops of water on the windowsill would never appear again. Some would lie where they fell all winter, while others would last no longer than a heartbeat.

The tailor shortened the focus of his eyes and found the image of his face in the glass. Instantly he turned away frowning. He could not look at his own likeness, as it was not the true reflection of who he really was and how he felt. He put his hand to his face, and covered his eyes and sighed.

'Well?' asked the candle maker, who had been watching the tailor from the door of the workshop. 'Are you coming?'

The tailor peered at the candle maker through the gaps between his fingers and spoke unhappily.

'What have you in mind?'

The candle maker went back to the workshop and shortly returned with human features that he had modelled in wax. He placed a long nose and a pointed chin on the tailor's face and fastened them around the back of his head with string. Then the boy entered with an old green overcoat with childish big buttons that no longer fitted him. He had a matching nightcap with a white woollen bobble on the end, and quickly he and the candle maker dressed the tailor and made him ready for the night ahead.

When they had finished, the candle maker and the boy examined the tailor from head to foot. After a few slight adjustments to his hat, and a quiet word to each other, they decided to roll up the sleeves of the coat a little, as they fell well beyond the length of the tailor's arms. Then they nodded in approval at their efforts and left the workshop to make their final preparations for the journey.

'Well done, my boy,' said the candle maker, as he loaded the last of the gifts onto the cart. Then he climbed aboard and began studying his list carefully, while waiting impatiently for the tailor to join him. As the boy returned to the cottage, the tailor finally appeared nervously at the door. After receiving a smile and a nod of encouragement from the boy, he cautiously approached the cart and took his seat next to the candle maker.

The sun was now setting, and the candle maker turned his head around and watched with narrowed eyes as it slowly fell below the horizon behind him.

'Make haste, boy, make haste!' he called out, and the boy rushed forward with a lighted spill from the fire and lit the lantern. He jumped clear of the cart just as the last of the sun was disappearing, and instantly the candle maker lifted the reins and let them fall on the horse's back.

The horse shot forward but no further than its harness would allow, as something was holding back the cart. The horse strained again but the cart would not move, and the candle maker and the boy looked around desperately to see what was stopping it. The candle maker examined the wheel below him, and the boy tried to push the cart from behind, but still it would not move an inch. Then the tailor noticed the obvious obstruction and tapped the candle maker calmly on the shoulder. He did so again, as the candle maker was so concerned that he may lose the night he had not felt a thing. The tailor slapped the candle maker several times on the back, but the candle maker waved him away until the tailor made his hand into a tight fist and hit him as if he was knocking on a door.

Eventually, the candle maker spun around and glared at the tailor with his face redder than ever.

The tailor sighed quietly then pointed to a wooden handle beside him that was locked fast against the opposite wheel. The candle maker's eyes widened in horror. Quickly he leant over and threw the brake. The cart shot forward, and the boy, who was still pushing from the rear, fell flat into the muddy patch where the cart had stood, which was uncovered with snow.

By the time the boy had sat up and wiped his face clear, the candle maker and the tailor were out of sight.

They had begun their wondrous journey. They travelled through village after village. They passed tiny hamlets and homes on the hillsides and in the valleys. They sped along country roads lined with cottages, and on through the market town, then further still to other villages where they had never been before, and always with the light from the lantern brightening everything where it fell.

The snow was deep, but the horse never slowed its pace. As they drove on, the candle maker and the tailor filled the little bags with gifts and handed them cheerfully to everyone that they met. They raced past houses, while the people inside hurried to their windows to see the great light pass outside. Some were too late to catch sight of the cart, but no one was left without something to say that it had called at their door.

In the streets people called out and waved to the candle maker and the tailor, without even knowing who they were or why they had come to visit their neighbourhood.

Some gasped in disbelief as the cart rolled by, while others stood rooted to the spot in surprise, holding their hands to their mouths and quietly laughing to themselves. Down the black narrow allies a bright light would suddenly burst into the passage and then vanish, while along the country roads that same light lit up the snowy landscape, as though the sun was shining on a hot summer's day.

At midnight the cart drew up to a short row of terraced cottages, where the candle maker slowed the cart and began filling the little bags with toys and candles to leave at each door. The tailor jumped down from his seat and hurriedly carried the bags to each cottage. When they reached the last home, the candle maker saw that there were no more bags in which to place the gifts. He looked sternly at the tailor, who simply shrugged his shoulders and turned away. The candle maker searched the cart but there was nothing there that he could see to use, so he pulled off one of his boots and removed his woollen stocking and filled that instead. The tailor placed the stocking by the door of the final cottage, then he leapt back onto the cart and they raced on again into the night.

***

By the early hours of the morning, the cart drew into an ancient village that might have stood for a thousand years. In its centre was a stone well, covered with snow and ivy, and the candle maker stopped the horse nearby to rest. Then he attended to the lantern, while the tailor examined the village.

Some faint lights flickered in the cottage windows, but across the street the shops and the alehouse with its little clock tower were closed. It was a peaceful village, tidy and neat, and the tailor thought that he might like to live in such a place if its people would accept him as one of their own. Then he nervously pulled at the candle maker's coat, as the cottage doors began to open and people made their way towards the cart. They also examined their village in amazement, which was covered with snow and now fully illuminated against the night sky. Cautiously, they crept forward, drawn towards the lantern like moths to a flame. The candle maker and the tailor moved to the rear of the cart, where they sat and handed out gifts to every villager.

For that short while the villagers forgot their troubles and differences, and they greeted each other warmly and fearlessly, even though it was the dead of night and the middle of winter. Then they brought out food and drink from their larders and shared their scarce resources with each other, believing that a little extravagance on one night of the year would not rob their supplies entirely and do good to themselves, their families and neighbours. The candle maker watched with a slight smile on his face as the villagers talked agreeably about the year that had past, and those who they had lost and others who had come into the world in that same time.

As they laughed together in the cold, an old man who was almost bent double with stiffness shuffled out of his cottage carrying a fiddle and bow. The villagers quietened and whispered to each other as he approached. When the old man reached the centre of the village, he smiled and nodded to the candle maker, who waved back at him, then he swung the fiddle under his chin and swiftly drew the bow across its strings. The villagers cheered and clapped their hands together in time with the music. Some broke out into a dance and pulled each other around by their arms.

The candle maker sat beaming on the cart, slapping a hand on his thigh, and even the tailor's foot began to rise and fall to the sound of the fiddle.

Then the old man began a new piece that was faster and merrier than the last, and the villagers responded likewise, as they recognised the music to a song that they had not heard for a long time. They joined hands and formed a ring around the well, dancing one way and then the other, while the village children made their own circle and their own dance to suit themselves.

The tailor bounced up and down in his seat, as he watched the villagers enjoying themselves. He turned and smiled to the candle maker, who suggested that he too might join in the dance. The tailor shrunk back in his seat at the thought and shook his head, but the village children soon dragged him off the cart, and shortly after he was leaping about among them in the snow.

The music filled the night air, and as the tailor danced with the children he forgot his unhappiness. Even when he noticed that his disguise had fallen off and was now hanging loose around his neck, he did not care because for the first time in years he felt himself and could behave as he wished around people. The children did not care who he was and saw him no differently from themselves, and the villagers, who had never seen him before to judge him unfairly, only saw someone who was pleasing their children, and that, in turn, pleased them.

The candle maker sat back from the scene and watched from the rear of the cart. Now he was the one who felt apart from the company. However, a young woman soon approached him bashfully with a garland that she had made from holly leaves. The candle maker bowed down towards her, thinking that she might want to whisper in his ear, but the woman simply placed the wreath on his head and quickly returned to her people. The candle maker sat up smiling below his crown and waved to the cheering villagers, who obviously approved of the woman's tribute. Then the clock above the alehouse struck the hour, and the candle maker and the tailor suddenly realised that they must say farewell to the villagers. The cart trundled off down the road with the candle maker smiling broadly, and the tailor chuckling aloud to himself for no reason whatsoever.

The horse was well rested and set a steady pace out of the village, where the road narrowed into a track and entered a wood. The night was not yet over, and so the candle maker and the tailor rode the cart further along the winding track and deeper into the trees towards their next encounter. They laughed and joked with each other about their journey so far, and, as they sped along the road, did not notice the snow becoming thicker below them or the wheels sliding on the frosty ground. Suddenly the cart rose up high on one side, the horse reared and the cart crashed to a halt in the snow.

The candle maker and the tailor climbed down solemnly and examined the damage. One of the wheels had run over a thick branch that was lying in the road, breaking its rim and smashing half the spokes beyond repair.

'Well, we can't go any further in this,' said the tailor, but the candle maker ignored him.

They had stopped before the shed of a woodcutter, and beside it were stacked long planks of timber that had been left out in the rain and warped in the heat of summer.

The candle maker walked silently towards the shed with an idea of how they could move the cart through the snow with only one good wheel. He inspected the planks carefully and selected one that was curved up at one end. Then he called to the tailor and they dragged the plank across the road, where they raised the cart with a few blocks of wood and fastened the plank under the broken wheel. When the candle maker and the tailor were back in their seats, the horse strained at its harness and the cart lurched forward. The plank slid easily across the snow, and soon they were travelling even quicker along the road, onward before the morning.

Nine

The following year the tailor decided that he would again join the candle maker on his round. Together they laboured for twelve months on the many different presents that they would give, while the boy ran the workshop alone and produced hundreds of candles each week.

In the spring, the candle maker scavenged the district, searching for anything that he thought might be useful. The essential items that he could not find he bought for a few shillings, but most of what he needed was lying neglected about the countryside or growing nearby. He collected wood and rags, glass jars and bottles, string and old packing boxes that no one wanted. Then he took them back to the cottage, where he shaped and painted them and turned them into gifts. He picked apricots, blueberries, strawberries and raspberries, and he boiled them up on the old stove to make jams. He dried cherries and tied them in little cloth pouches with brightly coloured ribbon. In the autumn, he collected apples and hops and turned them into cider and beer. He filled little pots with honey and mustard from the wood, and chopped wild vegetables and preserved them in vinegar to make pickles. He even baked a fruit pudding for an elderly woman in the village. As he stirred the thick mixture, he accidentally knocked a bag of salt into the pot by the fire where he kept his money. He returned most of the salt to its bag, but did not notice adding a sixpence with a pinch to the pudding. When the woman found the shiny silver coin in a spoonful, she took it to mean good fortune for the year ahead.

Meanwhile, the tailor worked at his loom. He weaved yards of cloth and coloured them with dyes made from kitchen waste, which he kept in buckets by the side of the cottage. Then he hung the cloth on lines that he tied between the surrounding trees, and, when the cloth was dry, he would sit in the sun and cut it and stitch, and remember the village where he had danced with the children. Yet the tailor never felt at ease outside the cottage. When anyone approached, he would quickly dart inside and hide in his corner, often trembling with fear until they had passed.

As the nights grew longer, the tailor became increasingly nervous about living in the candle maker's cottage. Sometimes people from the village would come and peer through the window, where the candle maker sat at his bench, curious to see what gifts he was making. Others would even knock at the door with their children, who usually asked for something special that year. The candle maker would listen politely but secretly preferred not to be disturbed, while the tailor longed for somewhere to work and rest his head in peace without fear of being discovered.

On the evening before their journey, the tailor sat by the fire and told the candle maker what was troubling him and what he had decided must be done. The candle maker listened carefully as the tailor said that he would take his belongings with him in the cart and, when they got to the village where the fiddler had

93

played, he would leave the candle maker to continue alone and settle there for the rest of his life.

The candle maker thought for a moment. He had seen the tailor change his mood in recent months but not thought it proper to ask why.

'I must say, you've been a great help to me this past year,' said the candle maker eventually. 'I'll be sorry to lose you,' he continued. 'But I'll not hold you here or stand in your way, if that's what you really wish.'

The tailor thanked the candle maker for his kindness. Then they toasted each other's health with mulled wine, and prided themselves on the good work that they had done and all that they had achieved together.

In the morning, however, they were not so merry. The candle maker had entered the stable early and found that the old horse was sweating up badly and too sick to travel. He had much to prepare, and so he gave the tailor some money and sent him out to buy another horse from the village or a nearby farm.

'Any kind,' called the candle maker, as the tailor hurried through the snow on his errand. 'Just make sure it's fast.'

The candle maker went back to the stable. He worried all day that the tailor might not find a horse before nightfall, but he went on loading the cart and carefully consulting his list while he worked.

It was an hour before sunset when the candle maker heard the tailor call out as he returned to the cottage. Immediately the candle maker ran out of the stable and found the tailor standing in the snow between two brown four-legged creatures.

'What do you think?' asked the tailor proudly. 'I bought two for the same price as one.'

'These aren't horses,' said the candle maker, and he studied the animals carefully through his spectacles.

'Well, what are they?' asked the tailor.

The candle maker sighed in disbelief.

'They're wild deer.'

'Seem pretty tame to me,' replied the tailor, stroking one of them on the forehead. 'The man I bought them from said he'd reared them himself. Anyway, they're all we have.'

The tailor was right. There was no time to search for another horse, as the sun was soon setting, so they quickly took the deer around to the stable, where they harnessed them to the cart.

The candle maker had made new spokes for the broken wheel and mended its rim during the summer. For the winter, however, he had fixed the cart on long curved wooden runners, as he remembered how easy it had been for the horse to pull it through snow the year before. The deer did not seem to mind the leather straps, but the candle maker doubted that they had the strength to even move the cart, let alone pull it for miles throughout the night. As he and the tailor returned to the cottage to make their final preparations, the candle maker reassured himself that if they only managed to get to the next village they might find a horse there that they could use instead.

'Now, don't fuss,' said candle maker, as he again fastened the tailor's disguise at the back of his head. 'It's only until you get there.'

'It tickles,' replied the tailor, but the candle maker was not listening. He poured them both a small glass of brandy, which had been a present from the boy's father, and they wished each other good fortune. As the sweet liquid warmed them both inside, the candle maker slung on the long red winter coat from behind the door, and they were off.

The deer trotted swiftly through the snow, while the candle maker nodded his approval to the tailor and agreed that the animals seemed perfectly suited to pull the cart. They were much smaller than the old horse, but together they were stronger and worked well beside each other, matching their footing through the snow. Furthermore, under the lantern, their coats shone like silver and reflected the light further from the cart than before. They may have seemed timid in the stable, but they did not fear the dark and now strode purposefully forward into the night.

The cart slid on, through villages, valleys and over hills, leaving gifts and good cheer in its wake. It would enter a district in silence and depart it ringing with happiness, which lasted the night through and could be heard for miles around. Seen from a distance, the cart was no more than a tiny white speck on the horizon, but within its bounds the light was almost blinding.

The candle maker and the tailor covered the same ground as the year before but in half the time.

'We'll stop a little further on and rest the deer,' said the candle maker. 'I know an elderly gentleman who lives on this road. Best I pop in and make sure he's well. He'll be pleased to see us, I'm certain.'

However, when they drew towards the old man's cottage, the candle maker grew worried as there was no light in the window.

'Hello!' cried the candle maker from the cart, then he turned to the tailor. 'He must be in on a night like this. Here, hold the reins. I have to make sure nothing's happened to him.'

The candle maker stepped down from the cart and

walked towards the cottage door, stroking his beard and beginning to fear the worst for the old man. He knocked on the door several times and called out again, but still there was no answer. The door was bolted and the windows were all firmly locked, so the candle maker peered through the glass, but the room inside was dark and there was no sign of life. Eventually, he returned to the cart and spoke to the tailor.

'I have to get in somehow. He may be sick – or worse.'

The tailor thought for a moment, examining the cottage. He looked from side to side, then his gaze rose up to the snow-covered roof and the broad chimney stack from which no smoke appeared.

'There you are,' said the tailor finally. 'That's the way in.'

'Up there!' exclaimed the candle maker. 'You must be mad.'

'It's the only way,' returned the tailor, and he jumped down from the cart and hurried towards the cottage, while the candle maker followed reluctantly behind.

At the rear of the cottage they found a ladder, which they rested against the side of the roof.

'I'm not sure about this,' said the candle maker nervously.

'Up you go,' returned the tailor, and he steadied the bottom of the ladder with his foot.

The candle maker looked up to the roof and swallowed anxiously. He held the ladder with both hands and began cautiously climbing the rungs. When he reached the top, he crawled over the roof towards the chimney, losing his footing only once but enough to send a shower of snow down onto the tailor, which almost buried him completely.

The candle maker looked down the chimney. There was no fire in the grate below, and so he squeezed himself inside and immediately disappeared into the blackness.

Inside the cottage two black leather riding boots suddenly crashed onto the coals.

'Aahh!' cried an elderly voice from the other side of the cottage.

The old man lit a candle by his bedside and found the candle maker sitting in the fireplace surrounded by a cloud of soot.

'What are you doing in there?' asked the old man.

'I was looking for you,' replied the candle maker, coughing heavily with his eyes streaming from the dust.

'I went to me bed.'

'Didn't you hear me outside?' asked the candle maker.

The old man looked guiltily at the half empty bottle of sherry by his bedside.

'Care for a snifter? Keep out the cold.'

The candle maker struggled to his feet and drank a glass with the old man. Then he reached into the pockets of the coat and gave the old man a bundle of candles and a jar of preserves. The old man thanked the candle maker and, as he walked unsteadily towards the door, he called after him laughing.

'I say. Why not drop in again next year?'

The candle maker was in no mood to reply and just grumbled to himself as he left the cottage.

'Wait till I tell the fellows in the tavern about you,' continued the old man, and he laughed aloud and poured himself another glass of sherry. 'Why, they won't believe me!'

'You look a sight,' said the tailor, when the candle maker returned to the cart, dusting off his coat and sneezing.

'Did you find him?' asked the tailor, but the candle maker simply climbed aboard in silence and drove them off down the road, not wishing to explain the experience, while the tailor giggled quietly to himself.

Shortly after midnight the candle maker suddenly pulled the cart to a stop beside a row of terraced cottages that he remembered from the year before. He looked closer and was surprised to see that woollen stockings had been hung out on all the doors. The candle maker did not even have to fill the little bags and hurried from one cottage to the next with a sack, putting gifts in every stocking. At the final door in the row, he found a small glass of brandy and a plate of cakes, which had obviously been left out for him. He drank the brandy out of sight of the tailor, but he shared the cakes with him when he was back on the cart.

As they drove off, a heavy shower of rain began. The candle maker and the tailor travelled about half a mile further, but they were forced to stop outside a solitary cottage on the road, where they pulled a tarpaulin sheet over the cart. The candle maker tied the sheet, while the tailor filled a bag with gifts to leave by the door. Then he stood thoughtfully in the pouring rain and pulled at the candle maker's coat.

'They'll be ruined if we leave them outside in this.'

The candle maker looked around, then he took the bag and hid it under the branches of a small pine tree that grew beside the cottage.

'How will they know the things are down there?' asked the tailor.

The candle maker thought desperately, then he pulled one of the little gold buttons off the coat and hung it ringing on a branch of the tree.

'If they see this, they'll know we've been,' said the candle maker. 'They'll look for them. Come on.'

They drove off again, and after a short while the rain eased then stopped altogether. The tailor lifted his bag of belongings from the back of the cart and set it at his feet. He smiled to the candle maker, who also recognised the road to the village where they had agreed that they would part company. The tailor began humming one of the tunes that the fiddler had played, while the candle maker sat pleased that his friend was happy but also sorry to leave him behind.

As they entered the village, the tailor picked up the candle maker's bell and began ringing it loudly. He expected to see the villagers hurrying from their cottages and come running towards the cart, but no one appeared. The candle maker slowed the cart as it approached the alehouse and took the bell from the tailor to silence its ringing. The time on the clock tower was wrong and the movement inside had stopped.

The candle maker and the tailor both stared in dismay at the buildings that lined the road on either side.

There was not one light in the whole village. The cottages had not been tended to for some time. The winter frost had cracked their windows and many of the doors had been left open, allowing the snow to drift inside. There were no footprints in the street, which was littered with unwanted belongings and children's playthings. By the well, the old man's fiddle lay on the ground, almost buried in the snow.

'What happened here?' asked the tailor. 'Where is everyone?'

The candle maker could not speak. He gazed in disbelief at the sight of the empty village, while his lips trembled fiercely, and not from the cold. The tailor solemnly removed his disguise, and together they drove on in silence and left the village to once more fall into complete darkness.

The candle maker and the tailor journeyed on for several miles without finding a single home to visit. The road became uneven and twisted down a hill, to where it ran beside a wide river. A few lights flickered on the opposite bank, but there were no houses by the roadside.

Neither the candle maker nor the tailor had ever been in this part of the country before and, although they wanted to call at the buildings opposite, there was no way to cross the water. As they continued, the river widened. The air became heavy and thick with a strange smell that made it difficult to breath, while the distant lights multiplied and now stretched along the whole bank.

'Poison,' whispered the tailor.

The candle maker stopped the cart and stood up. He listened carefully as a noise that sounded like a heart beating approached, growing louder. The light of the lantern fell out across the dark water, and in its beam a boat laden with goods appeared and passed close to the bank. A young man stood at its rear, while a boy shovelled coal into a large black oven with a tall chimney at its centre. They both turned and waved earnestly to the candle maker, who could only stare back in astonishment. The boat had a wheel on either side that churned the water and drove it forward, while from the chimney poured thick black smoke that filled the night sky and blotted out the moon.

The candle maker looked to the tailor, as if to ask if he knew what was powering this strange vessel, but the tailor was just as surprised to see a boat without sails moving steadily up stream. As the boat disappeared from the glare of the lantern, the candle maker realised that he did not know or understand the world that they had entered, but he felt that they must continue and see the night through, no matter what other mysterious sights they might witness.

The cart travelled further along the riverbank. There were sailboats moored to the other side, where men unloaded their cargo with cranes and brought it ashore. Then a great ship swung out of its dock and turned in the river. A tiny foreign voice aboard called out to the sailors, who were pulling at ropes to raise the ship's billowing canvas sheets a hundred feet high on the masts. The ship's boatswain, a huge man with a large white beard and a red woollen hat with a bobble on top, stood on the deck. He noticed the light on the shore and waved to the candle maker.

The tiny voice called again, and the men replied with their words bellowing through the cold night air.

'Way, haul away. We'll haul away, Joe!'

'Where are you bound?' shouted the candle maker, who was now standing in amazement on the cart and desperate to know more about the ship and its crew.

'Way, haul away. Oh haul away, Joe!'

'Where are you bound?'

'Round the world, man!' called the boatswain. He saw that his men had also noticed the candle maker, and they seemed to work all the better for doing so. They pulled at the ropes with greater energy, a sense of fellowship for each other and good cheer in their hearts for the voyage ahead. The boatswain raised his arm again and nodded agreeably to the candle maker, then he too returned to his work more purposefully than before.

At the ship's wheel the helmsman also saw the candle maker. Sitting beside him the ship's cabin boy waved delightedly towards the cart, while in his quarters at the stern of the ship the Captain and his officers crowded at the windows, and each raised a glass to the candle maker as the ship sailed off down river.

The candle maker sat down on the cart again beside the tailor. He was tired but knew that the night was not yet over, and they could still travel a little further before morning. As the cart moved on, they watched the buildings across the river grow higher and higher, and those beyond them spread out as far as they could see. They had reached the edge of the great city, and there came into view a huge brick building with many floors and dozens of barred and lighted windows. There was a low humming noise inside and plumes of black smoke pumped out from rows of chimneys on its roof.

The candle maker pulled the cart to a stop. He raised himself slowly to his feet and tried to imagine what purpose this living creature of a building might have in the world. Even from where he stood the air was choking and made his eyes water. The candle maker stared closer and saw something moving low in the windows, a few at first but then more, until almost every window held the same glistening scene. He looked carefully at one square of light and suddenly realised what was making it shimmer behind the glass and iron bars.

'Oh no,' he cried desperately, unable to believe the sight that lay before him. 'Oh my goodness me, no!'

The tailor also recognised the shapes in the windows, and now sat silent and mournful on the cart.

'No, it can't be!' exclaimed the candle maker, but his eyes did not betray him. The horror of what he saw was true enough. They were the children from the abandoned village, now locked up with hundreds like them and all waving cheerfully towards the cart from their prison across the river, where they were forced to work the great machines inside throughout the night.

Ten

The candle maker and the tailor returned to the cottage on the cart without a word passing between them. The journey had given them a lot to think about, and now they were occupied by their own separate thoughts. The tailor had not found a home, while the candle maker had realised what masses of people must live in a single city, let alone those in the whole country, or indeed the world. Furthermore, he had to accept that the world he knew as a child no longer existed, and in this new world there was a great deal that he did not understand. He regretted more than ever the years that he had spent locked away from other people, and he felt that if he had only known then what he knew now, he could have made better with his life. Nevertheless, such thoughts did not discourage him from his task, and he maintained that if he touched the lives of only a few more people than he had so far, at least in that, he could rest at peace with himself.

The tailor, however, was less sure of his future. In the early weeks of the following year, he did not leave the cottage once. Even before the winter's snow had melted, people from the village and beyond would come to knock on the candle maker's door and peer through his windows. They were only curious to see him at work, but the visits terrified the tailor, and, as they became more frequent, he decided that he could not live in the cottage any longer.

The candle maker also found the visitors distracting. He could not concentrate on his work when he knew that someone might appear at the cottage at any moment. Furthermore, the sight of the children in the factory had affected him deeply. He often sat in silent irritation by the fire and refused to speak to the tailor or the boy for hours at a time. Then he would find some fault with the boy and shout at him for no reason, other than to express his frustration with his powerlessness to change what he had seen.

One afternoon he entered the workshop and discovered the boy selling candles to one of the villagers.

'No!' screamed the candle maker, and he snatched the candles from the man. 'I forbid it!'

The man fled from the cottage in terror, while the boy tried to calm the candle maker. He assured him that there were enough candles for his next round and more besides to sell to anyone who might call in need of them. Then the boy took the candle maker by the arm and led him to the stable, where against the far wall he drew aside a curtain to reveal dozens of wooden boxes, piled high to the ceiling and filled to the brim with candles.

'When did you make these?' asked the candle maker.

'While you were sleeping,' replied the boy, a little ashamed of what he had accomplished without any help.

That evening the candle maker and the tailor sat by the fire, gazing into the flames and thinking the same thought. However, for a long time neither was able to speak their mind to the other.

It was clear that the boy, who was now a young man, could not only run the workshop alone, but also provide enough candles for the whole village throughout the year. Furthermore, it would be wrong of anyone to deny him a livelihood, which, given his abilities for the trade, would be sufficient to comfortably support himself and perhaps even a family. Yet the candle maker knew that such a business would only bring more people knocking on the cottage door. He was also aware of how unhappy the tailor was about living in the cottage, and he too felt uncomfortable with strangers watching him as he worked. Furthermore, the house that he had lived in all his life had not been a home to him since his wife had died, and so the only answer that would appear to suit all concerned was if he and the tailor found somewhere else to live.

'We'll move north,' he said finally.

The tailor looked up from the fire and nodded in agreement.

'Away from people,' continued the candle maker. 'We'll find somewhere ... solitary.'

Together they raised a glass to their new venture, and spent the rest of the night planning the move.

Over the next two days they loaded the cart with all that they would need in their new home. They packed what tools and materials the boy could spare from the workshop, and, by the afternoon of the third day, they were ready to leave. The cart stood outside the cottage overflowing with their belongings, and it was decided that they would leave the old horse with the boy and harness the deer instead, as they could also carry saddlebags on their backs.

The tailor climbed onto the cart and hid his face under a shawl. The candle maker said a long farewell to the boy, who thanked him for all his kindness and, if only to set the candle maker's mind at ease, forgave him for his occasional foolishness.

The snow had now thawed and the wheels of the cart trundled along the dirt road that led over the heath. They travelled for several days, through villages and towns, and along the country highways that weaved their way between green hills and ran beside clear rivers. Every so often, the candle maker spotted a piece of wood or a bottle or a piece of cloth that had been left by the road. The tailor would leap from the cart and quickly gather it up, and they would continue on their journey as though they had just stolen a fortune.

The candle maker and the tailor travelled both day and night. One took the reins while the other caught what little sleep he could, crammed in the back of the cart with all their possessions. They only stopped to rest the deer and cook their meals on an open fire.

Neither had any idea of how far it would be before they found somewhere to live, or what sort of dwelling they would eventually inhabit, but the candle maker reassured the tailor that there was a place for everyone in the world and all they had to do was continue until they had searched it out. They viewed every building that they passed as a possible new home. They saw cottages, lodges, barns and windmills, however, although many were promising, none seemed right for them both and the work that lay ahead.

Late one afternoon they drove through a small town with wooden buildings that lined the main street. It was not a homely town but one of those remote settlements where merchants, traders and travellers came to exchange their goods, replenish their supplies and rest up for a few days. The town had a provision store, a blacksmith's shop, stables and a small hotel, but none were in good order, and no one seemed interested in anyone's business but their own.

The candle maker and the tailor looked nervously at each other as they made their way through the town. However, although the street was crowded with people, somehow no one noticed either them or the cart, pulled by two forest deer, so busy were they at their work or with their own affairs. They drove on, both knowing that this town was no home for them, and yet the candle maker realised that such a place would have everything that he would ever need for his task that he could not find or make for himself. As they passed the last of the buildings, he looked back for a sign that would say what the settlement was called, so that he might return if necessary, but the town had no name.

The road climbed steeply and twisted across a barren landscape, where few trees grew and rocks lay exposed on the ground. On one side of the road the land spread out for miles, but on the other it seemed to stop abruptly, and from below there came a faint sloshing sound that fell on the ears like the slow beating of an enormous drum. The candle maker stopped the cart and walked cautiously towards what he discovered was the edge of a high cliff. The sun appeared low in the sky, and before it was something that the candle maker had only heard about but never seen before. He was further from his birthplace than he had ever been in his life, and he now stood shaking with fear and wonder as he gazed out towards the setting sun across a vast blue ocean.

The water crashed at the base of the cliff, and the candle maker thought that he could feel the rock beneath his feet shaking from each wave. The vibrations surged through his legs, which finally gave out, and he fell despairingly on his hands and knees, with his body exhausted from travelling and his mind overwhelmed by what he saw.

The tailor ran from the cart towards the candle maker. He placed his hand on his friend's shoulder as some comfort, but he could see that it was more than the strain of the journey that was troubling him.

The candle maker raised his head and look out through glazed eyes over the enormous stretch of rippling water.

'I never knew her,' he said finally, 'but I was told my mother came from across the sea.'

The tailor wanted to reply but did not know how, and so he just nodded caringly to the candle maker, hoping to say that he understood his sorrow.

'Somewhere far off, I believe. I don't know where.'

The candle maker gave a long faltering sigh but regained some of his composure.

'It's strange, life, isn't it?' he continued. 'The things you remember – all of a sudden.'

They both looked out over the wide ocean.

'We won't cross that in an open cart,' said the candle maker.

'There must be a way,' replied the tailor hopefully.

'Perhaps.'

The tailor waited patiently beside the candle maker until he was ready to continue their journey. Then he helped him to his feet and they walked back to the cart, where the candle maker lay down among their

110

belongings.

'You try too hard, that's your trouble,' scolded the tailor. 'Nobody gives as much as you.'

The candle maker did not hear him. He put his arms around himself to try and stop his shivering and began coughing painfully, as fever gripped his body like a vice. The tailor placed a small cushion for a pillow behind his head, and the candle maker closed his eyes, then slumped back against the side of the cart and covered himself with a shawl that he pulled up to his chin.

It was now dark, and the tailor lit a small lantern before he took the reins and drove the cart on into the unknown.

Suddenly a freezing wind blew up. Heavy rain lashed against the deer, but they struggled on, as though they knew the road and where they were heading.

The candle maker slept restlessly. The tailor worried that his friend might not survive the night, such was the worsening of his condition. There were no houses in sight, and no one about to ask for help, and so the tailor decided that they must return to the trading town, or else they would all perish in the wilderness. He pulled at the reins to stop the cart, but the deer would not halt or change their course, and even quickened their step with each jerk of the harness.

The tailor pulled harder at the reins. He called out, begging the deer to stop, but they would not give in and led the cart through a clump of trees, where there was not even a road, while a thunderstorm crashed above them.

The candle maker cried out in his sleep, as heavy

111

rain fell on his face and lightning bolted all around him. The tailor looked back in fright to see his suffering, but when he faced the front again, he could only sit back calmly in his seat with his forehead bleeding from a low branch that had struck him soundly. The blow had knocked out what strength that he had left in his body, and the tailor finally gave in to the deer and the storm and the pain, while the reins dropped from his fingers and he too fell into unconsciousness.

Eleven

The tailor slowly opened his eyes and saw the face of one of the deer staring knowingly back at him. He sat up in the seat, felt the bruise on his forehead, and found that the cart had stopped and it was now morning. Suddenly he remembered the events of the night before and quickly turned around to see the candle maker, who was obviously restored to health, lying in the back of the cart and snoring soundly, as though he was sleeping on a warm a feather bed.

'Oi,' said the tailor, and he nudged the candle maker on the shoulder.

The candle maker woke up.

'I think we're here.'

'Where?' asked the candle maker, sitting up and looking sleepily about him.

The tailor pointed to a solitary log cabin, which stood on an open meadow of spring flowers and was almost ringed with trees in the distance. The cabin had been built in the middle of a thick forest, but the trees nearby had all been felled and the wood removed, leaving only their stumps on the ground.

There were two large sheds beside the cabin, which would serve as a stable for the deer and a workshop for the candle maker, while on the main door hung a small painted sign that read simply 'Gone away', which meant that the previous owner had no use of the property and would not be returning.

'Yes,' said the candle maker, after a short glance at the property. 'This is the place. Come on.'

Together they unloaded the cart and began arranging the furniture that they had brought with them inside the cabin. Then they cleaned the stable for the deer and set about organising the workshop. As well as the candle maker's tools, there were some left hanging on the walls, and in the cabin there were a few cooking utensils and a black pot-bellied stove in its centre.

The candle maker hung the long red winter coat behind the door and placed his black leather riding boots by the fireplace. Then he set the brass hand bell in the centre of the mantle shelf, made a fire in the grate, and positioned his chair on one side and the tailor's stool on the other.

That evening they sat together content that they had made a place for themselves, where they could now work and rest without any fear of interruptions from outsiders. The candle maker opened a bottle of mulled wine, and they toasted each other's health and their new home. He purposefully filled his clay pipe with a fresh bowl of tobacco. Then he placed his spectacles on his nose, pulled out a bundle of papers from the side of his chair and, with a charcoal stick that he produced from behind his ear, began a new list for his next round.

Throughout that year the candle maker and the tailor worked as they had never done before. The candle maker made hundreds of wooden toys. So many, in fact, that they soon filled the workshop, while the rest he stored around the cabin. He had the boxes of candles that the boy had given him, but the candle maker still made his own, the smallest of which he used to brighten the insides of little ornaments and turn their moving parts with heat from the flames.

There was always some mixture or other bubbling fiercely on the stove. The candle maker set aside a bench in the cabin for the cooking, bottling and packing of his fruit puddings, drink and preserves, which eventually filled the shelves of an entire wall. Meanwhile, the tailor sat weaving at his loom or stitching by the fire. In the warmer months, he worked outside. He gathered berries, plants and flowers from the meadow and the wood beyond to make dyes, and he coloured his cloth with every shade of the rainbow. Then he sewed the pieces together to make curtains, pillows and bed linen for the cabin, as well as many large sacks, which he filled to overflowing with masses of cloth toys.

This year, however, the candle maker had even greater plans on his mind. He drew dozens of sketches at his workbench, and made thousands of measurements and calculations. He left no problem unresolved or detail overlooked, but the scale of the project that he was planning was huge, and sometimes he doubted that he could build what he now needed to truly fulfil his mission.

When the tailor saw him screw up yet another piece of paper and throw it despairingly at a pile of others on the floor, he cautiously entered the workshop and approached the candle maker's bench. The candle maker was reluctant to share his idea with the tailor, fearing that he might laugh at him or scold him for wasting time on such a bold and fanciful endeavour. Nevertheless, although he believed in what he was doing, he knew that he did not have all the skills to complete what he had so far only imagined on paper. Therefore, without any persuasion by the tailor, the candle maker hesitantly beckoned him forward to view his drawings.

The tailor studied the plans carefully. He rubbed his chin and shook his head, while tut-tutting noisily to himself. Then he took a sharp intake of breath through his tightened lips, and the candle maker sighed and turned away, wishing that he had never let the little man anywhere near his designs.

'There are only two weeks to mid-winter,' said the tailor finally.

'Less than that,' replied the candle maker.

'Well, we'd better get a move on, hadn't we?' returned the tailor, and he swept up the drawings in his arms and hurried out of the workshop towards his loom in the cabin.

The candle maker sat wide-eyed for a moment, then he shook himself irritably.

'Yes,' he called through to the tailor. 'Yes, we'd better!'

For the next few days the candle maker could be heard furiously sawing wood into planks and hammering them together in his workshop. The tailor, meanwhile, worked at his loom and weaved his finest cloth. He also cut pieces of leather, which he sewed together to make long strips, and added buckles and fasteners along their length.

The days were growing shorter and colder, but still the candle maker and the tailor worked on in secret, hidden from the world and its people.

One frosty morning the tailor entered the stable with a bucket to feed the deer. He was tired, having worked most of the night, and yawned sleepily. Suddenly, to his horror, he noticed that the stable door had been left open throughout the night. He called out to the candle maker, who hurried inside and found that the deer had not escaped, but now stood calmly with six others, which had wandered in from the nearby woods to keep warm beside their fellow creatures.

'They seem to like each other's company,' said the tailor.

The candle maker stood speechless at the sight that met him. He walked slowly forward and examined the deer carefully. They were all the same animal but, just like people, each seemed to have a different way about them. Some were quite timid and shy, while others were more bold and forthright, and the candle maker could see that what weakness there might be in one would be made up for by the strengths of the rest. They would work well as a team, but the candle maker knew that he could not force them to stay, and so he took the tailor aside and told him to feed them all and make them as comfortable as possible.

The next day the tailor harnessed two of the deer to the cart and prepared to journey down to the trading town for more supplies. The candle maker gave him a long list of all that they needed, and, although he was unknown in the district, the tailor left with his head hidden under a shawl and drawn tight across his chin.

The candle maker returned to his carpentry. He began laying out the wooden pieces that he had made outside, under the shelter of the workshop. He hung a canvas screen from the shelter and around the pieces, to protect them from the cold and wet. Then he went inside the closed and covered area with a light and a bag of tools to assemble the parts.

Meanwhile, the tailor had arrived at the trading town. He drove nervously along the main street with his face covered by the shawl, but again no one seemed to notice him or cared why he was there. The town was alive with people and yet there appeared to be little life in the place. Most of the inhabitants had a cold look in their eyes and little warmth in their hearts.

The tailor gave his list and a handful of coins to the keeper of the provisions store, and together they loaded the cart with all the sacks and boxes of goods that were required.

At the blacksmith's, the tailor showed the farrier one of the candle maker's sketches. Without knowing, or even asking, for what purpose they were needed, the forge was blasted with bellows, and soon long lengths of iron were hammered out on an anvil and twisted into shape.

The tailor was pleased with the work. He paid well for his two pieces of iron, which the farrier's apprentice loaded onto the cart. However, as he tied the tarpaulin, the tailor felt a cold evening wind blow up. He heard cruel laughter in the air and a faint roll of thunder in the distance, which unnerved him terribly.

'Impossible,' called a voice from outside the hotel. The tailor tried to ignore the outburst and continue with his work, but then came another.

'I've never heard such rubbish in all me life.'

Slowly, the tailor turned to see a group of men arguing across the street.

'They say he travels like the wind,' said a young man, whose son was having the same quarrel with an older boy nearby. The other men laughed drunkenly at the young man, while one poked him in the stomach with his cane.

'I know people who have seen him,' insisted the young man, but the others only laughed louder and teased him all the more.

'Poppycock!' cried one.

'Balderdash!' shouted another.

'Fiddlesticks!' called a third.

At the same time, the older boy had scolded the young man's son to the point of tears and was now yelling angrily at him.

'My dad says there's no such person.'

'There is, I say!' cried the child firmly, but the older boy just pushed him on his seat in the mud.

'Ha!' he shouted and joined the group of men by the hotel, who clapped him triumphantly on the back.

The tailor watched as the young man helped his son to his feet, and they walked soulfully away to calls of ridicule from the men and the sound of mocking laughter.

The tailor finished tying the ropes and noticed that his hands were shaking with fear. He drove the cart out of the town, feeling guilty that he had said nothing during the argument. He knew that he could easily have spoken up for the young man and his son, but he did not want to delay his mission, and his word, like theirs, would have offered no evidence to change the opinions of such doubters. In addition, he wondered how many other people there were who held the same view.

The tailor drove on into the night, and by morning he arrived back at the cabin. As he drew the cart to a halt, the candle maker emerged in a paint-spattered apron from behind the canvas screen with a bucket in one hand and a brush in the other. He wiped his forehead with the back of his wrist and left a smear of

119

red paint across his brow.

'Like the colour?' he asked proudly.

'It looks like there's more on you than there is on that thing in there,' replied the tailor.

The candle maker's face fell a little.

'Well, what have *you* been up to?' he asked.

The tailor untied the ropes and threw back the tarpaulin to reveal what he had bought. The candle maker's eyes widened when he saw the two pieces of ironwork, and he ran his hand over their curves before lifting them from the cart and carrying them behind the canvas screen. The tailor unloaded the rest of the cart and took the supplies into the cabin. He spent the day writing little labels and ticking the items off the candle maker's long list. Then he threaded the labels with string and tied them around each gift before carefully placing them into large red sacks, which eventually overflowed with brightly coloured presents. The tailor worked throughout the night and did not notice the first snow of winter gently falling past the cabin window. Meanwhile, the candle maker remained outside, working behind the canvas screen.

Early next morning, the tailor dragged the sacks through the snow to the side of the cabin, where the candle maker took them inside the covered shelter. When they had finished, they stood for a moment and looked out over the flat snow-covered meadow, which had frozen to solid ice during the night. After a moment's thought, they nodded to each other that everything was in order and returned to the cabin, where the candle maker rested for a few hours before his journey.

The tailor, however, could not sleep and sat all day brooding by the fire. His anxiety was made all the worse by the loud peaceful snoring that was sounding forth from the other side of the cabin.

When the candle maker woke, he washed, combed his hair and beard, and changed his clothes. Then he unpacked a brown paper parcel from the provisions store, and he stood for a while admiring himself and his new red britches in a long mirror, unaware of the tailor's concern.

The candle maker pulled on his black leather riding boots and sat comfortably in his chair by the fire. He lit his pipe and poured two glasses of mulled wine, but still the tailor sat gazing silently into the flames.

'Won't you join me?' asked the candle maker.

The tailor looked around worriedly and saw the candle maker smiling beside him and offering a glass in his outstretched hand. The tailor solemnly turned back to the fire.

'What is it?' asked the candle maker.

The tailor did not want to say what was troubling him, but he cared too much for the candle maker to let him leave on his journey without knowing what he might encounter. The tailor turned his head a little to one side. He could not look the candle maker in the eye but spoke bluntly.

'I've heard people say they don't believe in you.'

The candle maker sat upright in his seat and looked sternly at the tailor.

'What people? Who says this?'

'They say there's no such thing as you,' continued the tailor.

The candle maker placed his glass aside in a state of astonishment and confusion. He slowly rose to his feet, unable to understand what he was hearing.

'No such thing!' exclaimed the candle maker.

'What do they mean?'

The tailor wished that he had not spoken but now felt that he must tell the candle maker everything that he knew about the doubters in the trading town.

'They ask how can you visit so many homes in one night?'

'You'd be surprised what you can do in a night,' returned the candle maker.

'They say you don't exist!' snapped the tailor.

'Of course I exist. I'm here, aren't I?'

'I know that,' said the tailor, retreating back on his stool and allowing the candle maker a moment to think over what he had heard.

The candle maker moved uncertainly, turning from side to side, then he shrugged off the suggestion and spoke firmly to the tailor.

'Confound them, I say. I do exist. I'll show them I exist.' Then his voice rose sharply, 'Why, I'll visit every home in this land tonight. I'll visit every home in the world!'

'How?' argued the tailor. 'How can you visit every home in the world in one night?'

The candle maker shouted back furiously, 'Because I am already there!'

He calmed himself but was still shaken from the thought that anyone should question his ability to accomplish what he had now made his life's work. Then he continued, explaining his motives as much to himself as to the tailor.

'If people know of me and think of me for only one night of the year, then I am among them. It's the spirit of the thing that counts. Nobody gives a thought for candles in any other season, but in winter ... Huh!'

Then he spoke firmly and addressed the world in

general.

'Let them say what they like about me. Let them doubt me. Let them deny me. But let they who choose to do so believe in me!'

With that, he seized the long red winter coat from behind the door and strode out of the cottage, purposefully into the cold.

The sun was falling in the sky. The candle maker carried a heavy harness over his shoulder to the covered shelter, where he laid it out in two long lengths on the snow. He was still annoyed with what the tailor had said and muttered crossly to himself as he worked.

'Don't believe in me. What rot! He's a fool, that tailor.'

The candle maker then went to the stable and led the deer out, and harnessed them in two rows of four. Then he took the end of the harness into the shelter, where soon streams of light shone out from below and through holes in the canvas screen.

The deer waited patiently for the candle maker to return. When he did, he led them slowly forward, and they pulled out from the shelter what he had been making, which finally broke through the canvas screen and came to rest outside on the snow. It was a great sleigh.

The sleigh was freshly painted in red with gold trim, and decorated with sparkling silver stars and golden sunbeams. It was heavily laden with dozens of sacks, filled with candles and colourful gifts. The iron runners curved up high at the front and slid easily on the frozen ground. The seat was padded velvet, and there were soft cushions of the same made by the tailor, while above a great lantern shone out over the deer, and far beyond, to create a ball of light that was bright as the sun.

The candle maker halted the deer. He checked the harness, still grumbling stubbornly to himself, but, as the sky grew darker and a cold wind picked up around him, he looked out across the snow towards the trees in the distance and suddenly felt terribly frightened and alone.

'No such thing as me,' he whispered despairingly. Suddenly he understood the full extent of what the tailor had told him. He thought anxiously for a moment, feeling a little foolish with himself and his strange appearance.

'Why,' he stammered with a lump in his throat, 'I can't do it if they don't believe in me. It's what gives me the strength, drives me forward. Without them ... I'd be nothing.'

The candle maker turned to the lead deer. He glanced bashfully into its eyes as he spoke, wishing for some words of encouragement but knowing that the animal could not reply.

'Do you think people still believe in me?'

The candle maker looked up as stars appeared in the sky overhead.

'They ought to have something to believe in.' Then he slowly returned his gaze to earth.

'There was once someone who believed in me,' he continued. 'But now I'm not so sure.

'We've been away many months now, out here,' he went on, thinking aloud that perhaps he should not again have hidden himself from the world, and that, at least, when he lived among people, he remained in their thoughts and could not be disproved.

'Perhaps they've forgotten all about us.'

The candle maker again looked to the lead deer for some support. 'People do, you know? Forget.'

The sun fell below the horizon and the sky turned black. The candle maker stared mournfully across the empty meadow and realised the possibility of an unbearable truth, while the full horror of what it meant to his fellow beings appeared across his face.

'What must they be like now,' he whispered. 'After all this time, living in darkness – with nothing to believe in?'

The candle maker now feared the journey ahead. He thought that he should return to the cabin, where it was warm and safe. However, he knew that he must find out for himself what people really thought of him, and he still felt compelled to venture forward into the night.

'We all need someone to believe in us,' he said, as he decided that he could not abandon his task. Yet before he set off he made a firm vow to himself.

'If they don't believe in me after this night, I shall disappear from their lives forever.'

The candle maker turned away and thought sadly.

'We shall know by the morning.'

He climbed wearily aboard the sleigh and nervously picked up the reins. Then he looked out over the snow-covered landscape and spoke brokenly with frozen breath through his great white beard to the cold night air.

'Is there one soul left in this world who still believes in me?'

With his hands trembling, he slapped the reins on the lead deer's back and at that moment the candle maker, the sleigh and the deer suddenly vanished from the spot where they stood.

Twelve

The deer's hooves raced across the ice faster than they had ever run before. Faster and faster they trod, pulling the sleigh with unbelievable power, as though it weighed nothing at all, as though it were no longer touching the ground, driven forward by some invisible force towards the homes in villages, towns and cities – everywhere.

Faster still the deer ran, leaping yards with every stride, galloping further into the night. Miles, it seemed, went by in a second, and mile after mile they covered without faltering a single step, each in time with the others.

The candle maker struggled with the reins, trying to pace the deer for the long journey ahead, but nothing would slow them. He cried out, scared and confused, unable to understand the force that was driving them, and he held on for his life, frightened that he might be thrown from the sleigh at any moment.

The great ball of light in which they travelled shot across the countryside and spun out into a long bright tail behind them, as if the deer were running swifter than the eye could see and faster than the light itself.

They flew past the doubters in the trading town, scattering snow in their faces.

'Well, I'll be blowed,' shouted one. 'It is him!'

Another looked dumbly at the bottle that he held to see if the drink had affected his senses.

And still the deer sped on, soaring over snow-covered hills and through valleys. Quick as a flash they darted down streets, so swift that some people missed their passing, while others stood dumfounded at the sight that they witnessed.

The candle maker shook with fear and closed his eyes in terror. The cold wind blew in his face, ruffling his beard, and he moaned loudly, pleading with the deer to ease, but they galloped on despite his cries.

Then a sound approached that the candle maker recognised. It was distant and faint at first, but as the sound grew louder he calmed and dared to open his eyes.

What the candle maker saw made him realise that he should not fight the deer any longer but let them run. He saw crowds of people on every road and street. In the villages and towns hundreds were gathered, and in the cities there were thousands. The sound that they made was like a great wave on which the candle maker rode, and a wave that he felt sure could take him anywhere. The people were cheering him.

Some clapped their hands together, quite overcome by the moment, while others smiled, laughed or roared with pleasure when candle maker went by. Wherever he travelled people had heard of the candle maker and were waiting to see him, and the joy that they felt in their hearts when he passed made him feel young again.

'Bless my soul!' cried one woman.

Church bells rang out at his coming. The sick rose from their beds. Children's faces beamed in wonder and delight, while those sleeping soundly dreamed that the candle maker would visit them that night.

There were presents, special treats, pine trees with decorations hung on their branches, great feasts laid out in every home, music, singing, dancing and rejoicing, but most of all lights. There were lights everywhere.

The candle maker sat on the sleigh in astonishment. He began shaking again, not in fright this time but from surprise. His lips trembled, and he spoke quietly to begin with, scarcely able to utter the words that he now knew were true.

'They believe,' he said. 'They do believe.' His voice grew louder with excitement. 'They believe in me!'

The candle maker sailed on into the night, shouting out to the world from high up on his seat, while below the people cheered him all the more and were showered with gifts from the sleigh.

'They believe in me!' he called again. 'By Jove, they believe in *me*!' and he laughed uncontrollably, while his voice boomed out far and wide across the whole night sky, 'Ho! Ho! Ho!'